The Adventures of Nagel

of Ancient Babylonia

By Wilma R. Forester

Order this book online at www.trafford.com
or email orders@trafford.com

Most Trafford titles are also available at major online book retailers.

Printed in the United States of America.

ISBN: 978-1-4269-8238-5 (sc)
ISBN: 978-1-4269-8239-2 (e)

Trafford rev. 08/02/2011

 www.trafford.com

North America & international
toll-free: 1 888 232 4444 (USA & Canada)
phone: 250 383 6864 ♦ fax: 812 355 4082

Preface

The needs and desires of the human spirit are very much the same the world over, no matter what age you were born. This book of course is fiction. I couldn't have known Nagel. However, I have researched the time, location, and culture and attempted to make it fit as if I was there.

The triumph of the human spirit is ageless. If we could magically look back in time, you may have to change the name but I believe Nagel was there!

This book is dedicated to my sons, grandsons and great grandsons and the free-spirit of young boys and girls the world over.

Wilma R. Forester

Chapter One

Once upon a time a boy named Nagel came for his spin on the earth. God sent him to the land of ancient Babylonia. The time in history as we count time was about 1400 BC. Research has shown this cradle of civilization, as it has been called, had a surprisingly advanced culture. The Empire of Babylon reached from the Mediterranean Sea on the west, the Caspian Sea in the north the Red sea on the south, and the Persian Gulf on the Eastern corner and covering several thousand miles. However Nagel would say he was not really a Babylonian. He would say he was NOBODY from Nowhere!

"Nagel, you have deceived me, you promised to do your work and then you ran away. Why should I just take you back? You know what happens to low class runaway slaves like you!" Master Armen raged at him. Nagel's naturally tan face turned white. He had never seen Master angrier. Nagel tried to keep his voice low and calm. His fate could be sealed with a wave of master's hand. He knelt down crossing his arms on his chest and lowered his head. In Babylon in the city of Nippur, the culture taught it was the ultimate show of respect to do so and the higher the authority the greater the prodigal and NOW was the time to show respect!

"I am sorry sir I never meant to lie to you," he replied in rather small voice. "I ran away because I could not work any faster, the water jars were too heavy, I just couldn't lift them any more and I was afraid Master Gates would whip me." He knew he wasn't really that abused but the trouble with trouble is it always starts out like fun. Being free from his day after day heavy work load was scary and exhilaratingly wonderful at the same time, even if he had been caught, it had been worth the risk but not if he must DIE for it!

Master Armen started pacing back and forth his hand rubbing his chin thoughtfully, maybe he had expected too much from a little slave boy but he had to punish him and he wanted to teach him to be honest. He remembered this slave was a strange child of mystery. He glanced at Nagel standing there stiffly at attention, thinking this was the quiet one with hair too straight and his feet seemed too big for the rest of him. To the guardsmen he yelled, in a disgusted tone of voice "Take him away until I decide what to do with him!"

The young boy Nagel was roughly taken down stairs and outside to a dark and dingy den of confinement. "Gates," he demanded, "you are the one in charge of this slave. Where did you find him and what is going on here?" Master Gates was a rather quiet impatient older man with long gray hair tied up on the back of his skinny neck. His long face matched his serious disposition, he had not a kind word for anybody much less a slave boy like Nagel but he held a position of high authority in Master Armen's Estate and not much happened without his being involved in it.

"Master Armen sir," began Gates while bowing deeply, "he was hiding in the streets of Nippur. He seems to have friends there, as well as lots of kids to play with. I am afraid he is too young to do all that watering and lift those jars by himself. He is kind of skinny and he doesn't listen to what I tell him to do, anyway nobody knows how old he is or where he came from and I Sir, I have been working elsewhere and have not had time to train him, but Sir," he continued, "as far as I know he is not a bad kid."

In the dark Negal felt along the mossy wall and pulled himself into a sitting position. "So I don't listen but at least I am not a bad kid." If he could just find the door he would like to pound on it and scream but his eyes had not adjusted to the dark, so he sat on the cold stone floor feeling very alone, at least he hoped he was alone. He felt angry and afraid and like a Nobody again. *What he didn't know is we are all always alone, we live inside our own minds looking out into our own world with our five senses but does anybody really knows our true thoughts or feelings, even when we try hard to explain them. If so, who?*

"Bring Nagel back in here," yelled Master Armen. "I am going to do something different this time but YOU (looking at Master Gates) had better watch over him and teach him what we expect from slaves around here!" He turned suddenly with anger still showing in his intrusive face. He pulled the trembling little boy to a standing position and looking him closely in the eyes, he said, "I am going to let you off this time but I want you to swear by all the gods of the Euphrates River you will never run away again."

What was I supposed to do, thought Nagel? He could not put his feelings of emptiness into words. Secretly inside he was glad he was a little cute and small of stature maybe that would save his neck, because when a run-away slave was captured death was the usual answer. He stood there trying to look innocent. Would it work? Master Armen pulled him in close and tilted his chin up and looked him in the eyes a second time and said, "PROMISE ME you will NEVER run away again!"

"Yes, yes SIR Master Armen, I PROMISE!" there came a shrill but grateful reply.

If this were a movie, the music would be a slow drum roll alternating with a suspenseful violin melody.

This was the beginning of a special agreement between a slave boy and his wise master… *Half the truth is a great lie and who can bear it?…* The real truth being, if Nagel ran away again, Master Armen would have a very small chance to ever find him. If he really felt that burdened with the work he would find some way to escape. The verbal contract that they finally settled on was this: Nagel would work for him Saturday through Tuesday night and if he did his best in all his jobs, he was FREE to go until the next Saturday morning. So he became a part time slave boy. If he kept his word he would be living in two completely different worlds. Would he or even could he keep his promise? He didn't know it now but someday Master Armen would have an important PROMISE to keep to him... *A small performance is always worth much more than a large amount of promise...*

Nagel felt very different from the people of Nippur but he wasn't sure how or why. Try as he might he had no memories of having a family or home. Here in this huge city in the Empire of Babylonia he was known as a just a ragged street boy on (Wed.-Sat. morning) but he also worked as a slave in Commander Armen's Estate (Sat.-Tues. night). This was a large, highly privileged family with a palace like home. It was a small city to itself, with its own workers, merchant and slaves coming and going. To really understand this story you will need to know how the people lived and what the land and culture was like, and more important, what was Nagel like and who was he? We could start with a very common type off living in the streets of Nippur, morning for him... *Music, fast light busy city rhythm...*

Nagel's city life

Early dawn is breaking. The sounds of the street below woke him before the sun was up. He lay in his ragged woolen blanket and listened. The burros and oxen that were stalled nearby and almost beneath him were calling for their morning hay and corn. "Dirty lizards, it's time to get up!" He said to himself. Even in this dim light, venders and travelers were already passing down the much traveled and worn brick street. The click, clatter of the animals' feet on the stone had almost a musical sound. In fact some of the passers by sang as they went along. With mostly a rhythmic, steady beat type of songs, OOHH YOO-OOHH YOO where we go nobody knooows, OOHH-YOO-YOO! Some people when working lighten their labor with song however rude it sounded. It served the purpose of keeping each group bound together and a signal to the beasts of burden to keep a steady pace. Other travelers just hollered and cursed at their animals and some went silently along. Even at this early hour they were already too tired to complain about their lot in life. As Nagel still in bed, looked toward the river he remembered having that same disturbing DREAM again last night.

THE DREAM, Beautiful white feathers are swirling in the water some going under the fast moving current and some floating away and he running along the bank. Now he is desperately grabbing for them but the cottony feathers stay just out of reach. Then he is in the cold, dark, water swimming with all his might. Suddenly the feathers and his hands are all turning red. It always ended with a circle of faces all staring down at him and a searing pain in his back. Why would this dream disturb him so much and what did it mean? He didn't know.

Master Armen

Nagel

Chapter Two

Nippur was a very large busy city in the country of Babylonia, with a population of perhaps 100,000 or more people. Along with the usual sounds the city had a familiar aroma;… *in a book you can even add a smell…* it was a mixture of animals, hay and all the different kind of food being cooked in the open air by the street people. Then there was the mighty Euphrates River. It was about a half mile away but the canals with its merchants and boat people formed a network throughout the city. The Euphrates and the Tigres Rivers, called Twin Rivers, were just miles apart in places. The latter one ran swift and deep the former one wide and slow. If you needed to go down river fast take the Tigris and if you were fortunate to catch a westerly breeze sail back on the Euphrates. The daytime sounds, from where Nagel had his hideout, were a constant calling, banging, braying. Then there was the aroma in the air, it smelled fishy, musty, and a little damp and yet good, it all added to the mood of early morning in the heart of this busy city in the great Empire of Ancient Babylonia.

Right now Nagel was a little bit cold. His legs ached from lying on the hard stones that covered the edge of the walled archway behind the marketplace. This was his usual bed when he wasn't at the Armens' place. He had covered his sleeping spot with a soft, worn, reed matt but it still got very hard before morning. He was a tall lean boy about eight years old but nobody ever celebrated his birthdays. When and where he came from was unknown and besides, there was no one to care about it. He had light tan skin with large brown eyes. His thick longish hair was a lighter color then most of the other children. He had a thin sensitive face with very little change of expression, never laughing out loud and seldom smiling. He NEVER allowed himself to cry. His philosophy was to show no emotion and be quiet unless spoken to; this got him into less trouble, he found life easier that way…*"The whale only gets harpooned when he spouts."*…

He felt safe up here on this ledge, mostly because no one knew he was here. If you glanced up from the street it looked like someone left a pile of rags up there. The animals in their stalls beneath his private spot added some warmth on the cooler nights.

"Where is Marmoset?" She was his most precious possession or maybe second best. His Silver Whistle was by far the most amazing thing he had. Oh, here she comes with a chit-chatter and mouthful of nuts, spilling most of them out on his blanket. She often drove the venders crazy with her mooching and stealing of fruit and such. She was a small monkey. No one knew where she came from? Perhaps she had escaped from some traveling animal show; anyway the two lonesome outcasts had bonded with a common need to survive in a very lonely, rough city.

Nagel stood up and straightened his clothes and brushed his hair, yes he kept a hairbrush on the ledge here in his little hideout. His other treasures were quite a collection of things; marbles, pretty rocks, special sticks, a dried horned toad and etc., you know boy things. Here in this hideout it was all his private space. He was surprisingly tidy for having no one to tell him what to do. He was also surprisingly hungry, but he knew how to get a great breakfast. You got it from the street people. You had to look fairly clean or the trick wouldn't work. He knew how to do a lot of clever things, mostly because he had learned the hard way how to survive. There were lots of other homeless street children living here and there in the alleyways or down by the river. He choose to stay alone, he felt safer that way. Older boys could be bossy or take your things. He didn't like the idea of fighting to keep his things… He pictured himself standing straight and tall and staring down at the bigger bullies. "Listen punk these things are all mine so bug off and leave me alone" But he knew that would never happen. Besides being a Nobody, he wasn't very brave!

Babylon was an unlikely spot for the world's earliest civilization to have flowered. Builders here have little stone or wood for building. The vegetation is sparse except "in the spring" and in the six months of summer the temperature can reach 125 degrees. *"Desolation meets desolation"*. Babylonia and Assyria are cited often in the Old Testament. All that was needed to reap a rich harvest was a steady supply of water during the rest of the year. Irrigation was the secret; an extensive infrastructure of canals, ditches, and basins developed around 5000 BC. A herder or a farmer could produce more then he needed for the first time in human history. He could barter the surplus to others and people had time to develop different crafts; such as pottery, metalwork, textile, and service to the gods. So civilization - with its mixed blessings - was born and so was a boy named Nagel; the meaning of his name -THE SEEKER-

The tiny furry brown monkey, Marmoset ran ahead of Nagel, with her long tail dragging and then it went straight up. LOOK OUT she's decided to get into something. He was afraid someone would catch her or worse, even kill her some day because she jumped about and got into the rows of food and house wares, which were for sale or trade in the street market places. There were dates, hot peppers, corn, ceramic pots, clothes, hot barley cakes, figs, nuts; and so many other things. He walked on by until he smelled his favorite breakfast of hot barley cakes with raisins and if he worked it right he got a warm cup of goat's milk to go with it. Most of the venders knew or had seen him there many times before this morning. He didn't smile much but he would jump in and help with fire chips or setting up a table or even watching some of the small children while their mothers were busy cooking or selling their wares. He didn't wait to be asked for help, he knew how to muster up an innocent look and be extra polite. It had always worked for him. However, he never understood the TINY babies and never offered to watch any of them. "Why did everyone think they were so cute?" They always cry, burp, or worse mess their pants? It was not his thing. Soon he was offered a great breakfast. Often this was the only time of the day that he got all he wanted to eat. Now he sat on the back of a low, two-wheeled cart and shared some hot breakfast with mischievous Marmoset who had miraculously dodged everything thrown at her.

His friend Jarro gave him a toothy grin and said, "Good morning Nagel." How did Jarro do that, Jarro was BLIND and yet he knew you were there and who it was? Nagel remembered trying to sneak up on him but it didn't work because Jarro sensed he was there and even called him by name. Jarro was a special friend and Negal liked and admired him a lot. Most blind people stood with their head down and didn't look at you. Jarro's strange blue eyes continually searched you out. He was tall, straight and well muscled with big, strong hands. He even made his way down to the river to get the reeds he needed by himself. He made sandals of twisted reeds and laced them with leather straps and sold them on the street. He was not just another blind beggar. Jarro didn't beg.

Sometimes late in the evening when the street people gathered they played music, Jarro would sing in a deep mellow voice. Nagel loved to hear him singing. But now, Nagel didn't return the greeting instead he just touched Jarro's hand as he walked by, it was his way of saying hello. If you are really a Nobody it was better to be quiet just to look straight ahead and keep out of the way. When he looked at Jarro he often remembered a story told to him by someone in his past... It was about two young muskrats caught in a spring flood. They were trying to swim back up stream where they had been swept out of the nest by the rising waters... *The first one kept swimming with all his might AGAINST the current and soon went under. The second one turned and went WITH the flow, and using all his fading strength, pulled himself up on a branch and made it safely to shore. Was it fortune or luck or knowing how to fight the battle?*

"Jumping Catfish!" With a start Nagel suddenly realized, Jarro only came to sell his new wares on Saturday. He had to be at the Armen's place early on Saturday morning or Gage would be angry with him. He could NOT break his promise to Master Armen. It wasn't very far away but it was a world apart and all uphill.

You could see the top of the tall beautiful brick buildings from the end of this very street. That was where he needed to be and quick! Everyone here knew where the Armen family lived because all of the rich first-class citizens lived over there. It was almost like a separate city. There was no time to try and jump on the back of some passing wagon and hitch a ride; he would just have to run for it. He shooed Marmoset away. She always stayed at the street hideout; it was safer for her here.

He began to run with his bare feet hitting the round stones of the road in a steady beat. He passed a group of ragged beggars some were crippled and another was blind like Jarro, what that would be like he couldn't stand to think about it. A world of darkness and then he remembered a song he had learned years ago. It went... My heart is sad to know of things you will never see; the blue of the sky, and the green of the grass, the trees Your eyes will never see the smile of a child or ocean waves in a gentle breeze. But your heart is sad to know I will never see, the images you hold deep inside of all the things so dear to you, will never be seen by me…. Imagination is not blind.

Marmoset

Jarro

So much sickness and sadness in a city like this, but there was joy also. He tried to think of better, happier things but just then he had to pass the Dark lane the trail that lead out to the dreaded place of priestly ceremonies and sacrifices. Horrible things happened out there. He shaded his eyes trying not to look that direction as he passed by, but it couldn't stop his thoughts. He knew the stories well of what the soldiers did to people who couldn't pay their bills, or sometimes it was because one of your neighbors didn't like you and passed rumors about you; or if you missed one of the religious ceremonies. To get in the way or even inconvenience an upper class person might well have fatal consequences. It could be a scary place with wandering animals and wild dogs.

He and some of the other beggar boys had gone there out of curiosity. They had seen a man being pulled down the street by mounted men, he was begging for mercy. What they did to that poor man, even watching from a distance made Nagel sick. The man received no mercy. Nagel never wanted to go out there again... *Go up to the burial and ruin heaps and walk around; look at the skulls of the lowly and the great. Which belongs to someone who did violence and evil and which to someone who did gallant and good?*

He rounded the corner breathless and with his heart pounding. Then he entered a beautiful more pleasant world. *Suddenly we have beautiful slow violins playing right here and you can imagine the variety of pleasant smells...* The long palm-tree lined lane lead him to high-even stonewalls surrounded and topped with trees and flowers. The wide wooden gates were hand carved and set with precious stones. It was the "The Armen Place." As Nagel approached he saw Erron the yard keeper opening the huge double wooden gates for the wagon of a sales merchant to enter. This was a very beautiful but private estate. Perhaps it was new garments for the ladies upstairs. Nagel burst thru unannounced along with the merchant's wagon. Erron frowned at him and gave a disapproving grunt but let him pass. Then the dogs started to bark fiercely at him. Why did they always do that? They knew him very well, they always had to bark and bark He felt that some day he might fall beneath them and be eaten up. He slowed his pace to pacify them. It worked and they calmed down. He continued, with several of the dogs still following him down the stone path with its colorful blue tile, through the flower garden around to the big back door, and into a large kitchen room.

Saturday morning was the time he needed to carry water to all the trees along the back fence, feed the dogs, bring in more animal dung chips for the fire and help Mirna or Gates with whatever else they wanted him to do. There was one job Nagel loved to do without being told. That was to help the trainer with the three beautiful stallions that were the prize possession of Master Armen. Nagel knew he was late and looked around nervously for Master Gates. Gates was the person that was in charge of him but it was Mirna who met him face-to-face, glaring at him.

"Where have you been? You are late! Lucky for you Master Gates is in a meeting with Master Armen, or you would have your hide tanned again." He didn't even try to explain. He hoped she would get to busy to mention his lateness to anyone. Gates had whipped him many times before even left lasting red marks on his legs.

He hurried out behind the kitchen area to get the earthen ceramic water Jars and start filling them. *Dreary working steady beat music here and the smell of sweat.* This was not a fun job. The water jars were heavy even when empty and when full he could not lift them no mater how hard he tried, so he used a flat stick to slide them up onto the steps. *"He who pours water hastily into a jar spills more then goes in."* There was a wooden cart to slide them into. The water was piped into the house from a cistern up on the hill. As he pulled the cart into place and groaned at his effort to slide the jars into the cart, he heard snickering behind him. It was Ahan the Master's youngest son. He was about a year older then Nagel. He was spoiled with too much attention, fine clothes and anything he wanted. However remember *potential is not a measure of success.* He was allowed to wander into any room in the whole place and check out what any one was doing. He seldom played with Nagel, but he often watched him from a distance while Nagel was working. Inside in his mind Nagel wanted to shout in anger at him. All the privileged first class children went to school several days a week; in fact the teacher came to the house… Now he was very large and tall and scowling down with a big frown on his face with all the other children cowering beneath him. "I will learn something too you will see, someday I will know everything even more then all of you!"… *Knowledge is like a ship which passes through the vast sea of time."*

There were so many things to know about. *"Kids have the natural desire and ability to learn!"* Nagel felt there might never be an opportunity for him to hear of these wondrous things being taught. As a Street boy and a slave, he knew the lowest class of all people was his lot in life, but your destiny can be rewritten. He would just have to figure out most things on his own. He knew the name Nagel means seeker or one who searches and it fit him well but most of the other children just called him the Kid from Nowhere. There was one thing Ahan had seen and wanted and had not obtained. It was the SILVER whistle! Just now Nagel slipped a hand up to make sure it was hidden under his tunic and out of Ahan's sight. It was Ahan's lies that made his life almost unbearable, saying he was not working when he was doing the best he could. Why would someone deliberately want to get you in trouble? He couldn't understand it when people lied and were mean to each other. Nagel knew that to be trusted is a greater compliment then to be loved. He wanted so much to be trusted and loved and to belong somewhere. It was all a part of the reason he had run away.

The day wore on and Nagel continued to feed and water and haul wood and fire chips. He was getting very tired already. I would love to stop and cool off and get something to eat, he thought, but I need to move even faster to make up for being late. Mirna called him into the kitchen to clean up the nutshells where she was working… *(God gives the nuts but He doesn't crack em!)…* Later in the day when most of his work was done, without saying anything she handed him a plate of food left over from last night. He slipped out on the porch to eat it and rest a moment. He heard the laughter of other children outside playing MakeMe. It was a game he loved to play.

MakeMe: You draw a circle big enough for six to ten children to stand on the outer edge of the circle. Try and make it on a hard, smooth, sandy spot. Color a smaller white circle in the center. The child in the center circle is IT. The children hold hand and form a circle around the outer circle and secretly pass the lucky stick. It is usually short, flat and painted red. The object of the game is to see if you can throw the stick in the center while running as fast as you can around the bigger circle and the It person tries to throw the stick back out, and he must hit the spot you were on with the stick before you can complete the circle back to your spot. If you don't make it you are IT.

Sometimes they played so hard; they fell down in a tangled pile of exhaustion and laughter. As he tried to see who was out there playing he felt resentful and left out. He thought about hiding the stick so they couldn't play next time but he knew he couldn't do it. Master Gates passed by and without saying a word smacked him on the leg for sitting down. Mirna saw it and gave Gates a dirty look.

Then with a shiver Nagel remembered one more important job he had to do. It was in the Mistress' bedroom upstairs. Nagel climbed up the twisting stairway of colorful baked tile to a large dimly lit bedroom lavishly furnished in heavy fabrics and massive hand carved furniture. He had a jar of fresh water and a large piece of raw meat in a basket. He knocked softly and pushed the huge wooden door open very slowly. He was glad no one was there, just Rajha. There she was, the weight of her long lithe body making a shadowy depression in the fabric above his head, with just her tail hanging over the end of the bed canopy. She did not move as he entered, just her yellow-green eyes watched and followed him. She was an Ocelot a treasured gift to the Armen family from King Mohad from the land of Ur across the River. Nagel had never seen such a beautiful creature not even in all of the parade of exotic animals sold by the merchant passing in the streets of Nippur. *If you play with a cat, you must not mind her scratch!*

He was not really afraid; it was more of an awe and wonder about her. He had seen her catch mice and rats moving like greased lighting when she wanted and she feared nothing, not even the dogs bothered her. He set the food and water in place and backed out of the room, leaving her alone. The room smelled like he might have to change her sand box. Oh well, later. She would not eat if he watched her too closely. The only thing that seemed to upset her was the occasional pigeons that landed on the bedroom window ledge. She would growl and hiss and slip under the bed until they were all gone. He wondered why she would be afraid of anything! The temple priests had all taught she was a mystical goddess to be worshiped. Didn't she have the power to curse or bless you? He didn't believe it and the Mistress must not believe it either, or why would she allow this wild creature to live in her own bedroom if it could put a curse on you? There were a lot of things he wondered about. … *Thoughtful light piano tones here…*

He had some deep thoughts about the difference between animals and people and even death and life and how life happened? It is the same questions we all have, where did he really come from? He knew he had existed before he came to this earth and he knew he had an inner soul. And when you look at the stars at night the wonder and majesty of it is overwhelming, it made him feel even smaller. What was the purpose of his life? What did it mean to be alive and what did it mean to die? The priest said… *(Life can only be understood backwards; but it must be lived forwards and every man must pass through much evil if he lives a long life)…* Nagel, even as young as he was, had already seen too much of life not to have a lot of questions. One day he had held an injured puppy as it died in the streets of Nippur. The wagon wheel of a heavy cart had smacked it. One minute it was jumping and playing and then he had watched as its life ran out. But where did that spark of LIFE go? It became a limp pile of meat. The puppy was gone! Even as it eyes glazed over, it wagged its tail one more time. Why do puppies love you even if you hurt them?…*Very slow sad melody here…* One grown lady sobbed and cried about it but Nagel didn't.

He had experienced too much of death and pain to let anything like the death of a puppy get to his feelings. That is what he told himself. Just don't let your emotions rule your feelings, (mister tough guy). This woman was really crying mostly for herself, perhaps SHE was afraid of death, he thought to himself.

He also knew where babies came from. He had helped the herders when the breeding season was on, sometimes you had to protect the prize bull, ram, or ass during the mating, especially when there was kicking and biting. Sometimes the animals were not very private about it. He had seen a lot of things most boys his age didn't know about. Also the street people did not hide too much from a young boy who often roamed in the night. Then there was the birth of things that was something to watch. There was the pain and strain of the mother and how she tried to be alone by herself for the birth. Cows, goats, camels, and sheep always rise up on their backend as the little critter drops, but ass's, and horses, rise up on the front end. The new little creature comes out wet and helpless but then the mother licks it dry and soon it stands to suckle her. He also knew that some animals were good mothers but some young inexperienced animals let their young die or even killed them. Where was his mother? Was there something wrong with him that made her not love him? … *Slow lonely kind of floating music here, please…*

Chapter Three

There was going to be a banquet tonight and there was a lot of extra work to be done. Mira and Gates worked him long and hard as well as themselves. Gates was in control of the whole front yard with its beautiful walkways and fountains. He was also responsible for the produce, corn, grain delivery and meat supply as well. He also did the butchering of the animals. Sometimes Nagel had to help and he hated the killing. Mirna was in charge of preparing the food. Nagel knew Mirna was the real boss of that whole end of the house. Mirna was a stocky, dark woman with her grayish black hair cut much too short for the long style of the Babylonian times. Her upper body was a bit too long for the length of her short legs. It caused her to walk funny and look a little bit tough. Nagel wished more people could be as caring and honest as Mirna. He knew her heart was very tender. But she could sure bark out orders to everyone around and if there was a problem to be solved you went to Mirna and not Gates.

"Nagel!" she called out loudly, "go and get more water and help me clean the kitchen, then you can go to the pool and clean up yourself!"

The pool, Ahhh, The POOL, he loved the pool. There was piped in clean hot water, a fountain of it, in the center of the house. In fact the house was built around it…. *Trickling piano notes like a waterfall sound here…..* The water continually sprayed into the center pool area and then flowed down over an alabaster stature of a huge lion with a man like head. The open ceiling revealed the usually clear, deep blue sky, and had smooth wooden colorfully painted supporting pillars. Most of the floor around it was rich deep green and red tile set into contrasting white, baked clay. There were larger then life- sized statues of different religious animal like gods set in nearly every corner of this large grand patio. With fragrant, lush flowers and long sweeping ferns in tall artfully painted ceramic pots, it all felt like a wonderful garden.

This was all completely wasted on a young slave boy. He noticed a cricket caught in the crack of a tile and found it much more entertaining. The pool usually had several people sitting around or in the water; but this time he had it all to himself. It felt wonderful to relax his tired, naked body in all that fresh hot water. Strangely enough he liked to be clean more than most eight year olds. He also loved white it was his favorite color to wear. Was it something in his background or some habit from earlier childhood? As he dried himself on the sunlight porch he remembered the strange mark on the small of his back. He had to twist around to see it, but now he felt it with his fingertips. Was it a scar or birthmark? He thought again about the DREAM, with the white feathers. The dream he couldn't understand. Where do you go when you dream and how do you get back? *Quiet no music here*

He wanted very much to stay up late on this special night and watch the festivities. There would be a lot of very important people coming to the Armen Palace tonight, with lots of food, fancy clothes, and loud music. Sometimes there were jugglers, dancers, even magicians, with trained, wild animals. Instead; he fell sound asleep on the back porch with the usual pile of warm dogs.

But on towards morning he awoke with the rustling sound of something outside in the yard towards the back wall. He was too curious to go back to sleep so he rolled out of his spot between the dogs and quietly snuck out to see what it was. Over by the grape vines he could see the outline of a tall, thin figure. This person was carrying a squirming bag under one arm? Nagel crept closer and watched the shadowy figure stretch out with the other hand and feel along the wall reaching up under the grapevines. Woops, where did he go? Nagel ran up closer to the wall being as quiet as he could on his tiptoes and looked under the tunnel of spidery grapevines where the figure had just a second ago disappeared. There he found a tall wooden gate hidden in the tangled mass. It had just been very silently closed. He waited a short while and then slid up the rusty latch on the gate and followed. The man ahead of him was half walking and half running as he hurried down the back pathway towards the poorer side of town. Then onto the gravelly road he went as Nagel continued to follow. It was still quite dark and Nagel had no shoes on. Then the man stooped to lay down the still squirming bag while he quickly lit a small wooden torch. Ouch, ouch, oh that was better. Nagel had to keep quiet and stay back behind this guy but he could see a little bit better now. Around the corner and down the road then the figure ducked into a shabby rundown little house. That had to be Gates, thought Nagel. His heart was pounding in the excitement of the chase, but what was strange, mean Master Gates doing and what was in that bag? Nagel just had to know so he slipped around to the backside of the little house and climbed up on some wooden steps and stretching so hard it hurt, he peeked into the window. If they had a big dog he was toast. It seemed they didn't.

An older white haired woman greeted the man and together they went into the bedroom. He placed the bag on the bed and pulled out a tiny white kitten. Then the man nudged to awaken the figure sleeping on the bed and showed him the cat. It was "Kinky" the white kitten with the crooked tail. All the kids loved to play with her. The boy rubbed his eyes and then he giggled out loud in delight at the beautiful little bundle of fur. The boy tried to talk but the words came out strange and Nagel could see his legs were twisted and he moved his body with great effort. Right now his own hands were slipping and the wooden steps began to creak so he quickly let go and ran up the street to hide. Nagel wasn't sure what he had seen and he thought about it a long time while he tried to find his way back home to the hideout. Who was that boy? Wow, this picture of unusual kindness didn't quite fit the image he had in his mind of mean old Master Gates.

The thought of returning back to Master Armen's estate through that vine covered, spider webbed gate in the dark was too much. So he began to follow the gravelly road back to Nippur.

He knew the way but it took all the courage he had to travel the road in almost total darkness. The thought of breaking his promise to never run away again worried him a bit because he knew it was a day too early to go to his hideout but most of the work was already done and maybe they wouldn't miss the Nobody kid. As he walked along he pictured himself grabbing mean old Master Gates by the front of his tunic and staring in his face while shouting… "I am not just a skinny nobody's untrainable kid. I belong somewhere and some one out there cares about me!" But the picture would not work. He was too short and even in his crazy thoughts he had to run and get a stool…

Somewhere across the Tigris River in the land of Ur there was a beautiful lady. She had been a widow. Now she stood staring at a flaming candle in deep thought. She was tall and slim with long light brown hair and hazel green eyes. Two years after her husband's death, she had married again and now had two young children. She could hear them playing outside the door of her home. It was the fifth anniversary of the tragedy that had changed her life forever. The day her husband had been killed and her son taken away. She prayed sincerely and often that her son might still be alive somewhere… *More slow violins here…*

She was the oldest child of a large family. She had fallen in love with a young handsome military man, and they married young. They soon had a fine son. Her husband was often away on long trips and she and the boy had a lot of wonderful extra time together. He was getting so tall and looked so handsome in the white tunic she had made for him. She had plans to teach him every thing she could at home and when he was older he could go to the temple and learn more about the world and all its wonders. Note: He, like other children of that time, would be taught mostly all about Astronomy and how to please the gods and that the life of an individual mattered very little so you must live to serve the rulers. She loved her four-year-old son so very much.

She watched the candlelight flicker and drank in its rich fragrance then her mind went back to that terrible morning… It was clear and cold that winter day but she and some of the other women with their young children had gone down to the river to wash their clothes as they usually did. Her husband came to watch out for their safety because there were rumors of roaming bandits. Exciting drum roll and battle sounds here. They heard the dogs fiercely barking. Then there was just confusion and screaming as several strange men attacked their group. The men were waving large knives, sharp spears, and shouting. She ran up the bank but their little boy ran towards the river, as her husband ran to protect their son he was killed with a thrust from a spear… *The music suddenly stops here…* The same spear cut into the lower back of the child.

Many people were killed and had their homes looted and burned that tragic day and several people like her son were just missing. The attackers fled in a riverboat going down stream. Clinging to a mooring rope of the fleeing boat was a small child with blood on his white tunic. She continued to stare at the flickering candle. She would always search through every crowd of people or group of children everywhere she went, forever looking for her son. She remembered each of his birthdays and she had saved his favorite toy, a tiny clay boat. She even kept his little sandals. Her heart ached to know what had happened to her son.

Wednesday morning came Nagel had worked long and hard during the four days at the Armen place and now he was free to go back to his street hideout. As he climbed on the back of the feed merchant's wagon and rode back toward the lower part of town, he sang a little song softly to himself… *Down in some green valley in a lonesome place, where the wild birds do whistle and their notes do increase farewell pretty Sara I bid you ado, but I'll dream of pretty Sara where ever I go …*

Mirna had given him a new yellow shirt with pants to match, and a nice breakfast to go. He really liked her. She had never deceived him! It was a warm sunny day and he felt good.

"Where is that rascal Marmoset?" He ran down towards the river to look for her. No monkey but there was a lot of shouting; barking and yelping from near the waters edge. Sometimes a crocodile wandered up the river canals and got to close to town. The street people didn't like the big ones, even though they were considered sacred. The men and boys would shout and throw rocks and if it didn't leave they would smack the water surface hard and loud with flat reeds and that usually sent them off. But this time it was a large shaggy mother dog that he had noticed before. She was behaving strangely. Nagel could see several of the street boys were down there throwing rocks and sticks at her. He wondered where were her pups?

There was a lot of roaming, stray dogs here and there throughout the city. They were just kind of wild and sometimes dangerous when in hungry packs. He ran down to check out what happened, but by then, the boys were playing in the water and swimming. He was glad to strip off his new clothes and join in the fun. He was a good swimmer and they played rough and rowdy all morning and late into the afternoon.

He spent the evening listening to the talk of the local men while sitting by the fire and passing food around, which he helped himself to… The only new thing in the world is History you don't know about… They had a lot of stories to tell, maybe true, maybe not. His blind, friend Jarro was there and Nagel loved to hear the adventures of the time when Jarro was young and could see. Everyone listened intensely because he had been an amour-bearing soldier in the army of King Llugalzaggesi. Serving as a mounted general in several battles, he had traveled to many strange lands. Tonight he spoke out softly, but it was a voice that some how filled the night and echoed crossed all barriers of history… *Time and chance at sometime comes to every man…*

"Once upon a time when I was a young man in the service of the King"…he leaned back in the chair, with his chin up, the light of the fire was flickering on his gray hair and beard, and glowing on his handsome face. His now unseeing blue eyes still shinning and all the past memories still locked in his sharp mind. He was a great storyteller and Nagel felt just like he had been there in these adventures right along with Jarro. He stayed up late and listened to all of it. He wanted to ask how he became blind but in his usual way, he kept quiet. Later that night, as he lay by himself in his hideout, Nagel could hear a lute being softly strummed and Jarro singing… *Lonely River in the moonlight winding through my song. Tell my love I am broken hearted lonely river flow on along…* Influence is directly related to intimacy and you can't love someone or something if you don't know them. He knew Jarro! It was very comforting to him. He slept well.

Marmoset woke him early the next morning. He wanted to pet her but she wouldn't hold still. She seemed agitated and wanted to go somewhere. He grabbed his shirt and pants but forgot his sandals and followed her down to the bank of the canal barefooted and hardly dressed. Sure enough she had something cornered in a muddy tunnel. Some days she spent all her time chasing the muskrats in the holes along the clay river banks.

"Get back Marmoset let me see what you've got," getting down on his knees messing up his new yellow pants he strained to see what it was. Two brown eyes peeked back at him. He got a bamboo stick and dug and prodded but to no avail. He could not get whatever it was to come out. After several hours he gave up and just set down. It was too late for breakfast. Marmoset had run off. He sat there a long time dreamily digging in the sand. When he looked back at the tunnel he jumped at the sight of a wet muddy puppy staring back at him. It was thin with a potbelly but had the most adorable face he had ever seen. There was no one to say he couldn't keep him.

After some coaxing and petting he wrapped it in his new yellow shirt and climbed up to his hideout home, using mostly one hand. It was such an effort, when he finally got up on the ledge of the hideout he was in a nervous sweat… *Light fast flute music here…* He tucked the puppy in his storage basket after quickly dumping the contents out and tied the lid shut. What if it jumped out and fell off the ledge? Hurry, oh hurry, get some warm goats milk and meat scraps. He never felt so excited or happy. He had his own puppy! He loved Marmoset but she belonged to everyone and would never stay very long with him. What should he name it? It seemed so very young and would it live without the mother? The puppy was just like him, alone and no one to care about it. When he returned with the food, the puppy had chewed its way out of the basket but he didn't go near the edge of the ledge.

Crazy Crocodiles! It wasn't only cute it was smart! They didn't sleep much that night.

When Nagel went to the Armen's place he had to take the puppy. He just couldn't leave it alone for four days. Saturday morning came and went with out much fuss over the new little creature. He did all that worrying for nothing. To Mirna and Gates it was just another dog to run around the place. "Just be sure to do your work without being distracted." Gates had demanded. Some of the other children (Ahan, Master Armen's son, had a sister and several young cousins) played with and watched over Nagel's dog while he was working. They all decided to call him "Scrappy." He thought that name fit real well. Ahan said he didn't want a dog that ugly… *(Like the fox that couldn't reach the grapes, so he said they were sour)… .* Nagel thought Scrappy was beautiful and he was happy that Ahan didn't like him. The winter had turned to spring and Nagel unknowingly passed another birthday. He moved his hideout down to a lower ledge so Scrappy could come and go easier and, of course, sleep with him. Marmoset and Scrappy got along well and even played together unless there was food to fight over.

Scrappy

Mirna

Chapter Four

A bit of history of the Empire and what the country was like here: there was much violence and raiding, burning and robbing on the countryside by neighboring tribes of people. The main cities were usually walled and guarded by the kings armed and mounted men, so people felt safer in their cities. They had beautiful buildings and towers called Ziggurats with large steps as the main structure on the outside. The sacred marriage vows and religious ceremony's were some of the many functions done there. The name Babylon may have come from the story in the Bible of the tower of Babel which could have been built in the shape of a Ziggurat. Also, the name of Babylon is mentioned four or five times in the Bible. There were statues and painted drawings and other fine works of art often of half-animal and half-human, these were lifelike, colorful, and well-done. Art was seen in blankets, rugs, tents, pottery and clothes. The linen cloth rivaled some woven today. They had blacksmiths with forges for jewelry, horseshoes and other metal needs such as weapons. The king of the Hittites, Hattushili said of Babylon, "*There are more horses even than straw.*" Fine horses came from the Kassites and were trained and breed in Nippur. Camels were rare and said to be one camel equals five Asses. Camels were called the ships of the dessert.

On several occasions' unusual races of people wandered into Nippur, like Mongoloid, Negroid, or Norsemen who rode on strange short-legged ponies. Many of them were herders or shepherds; some just roamed the land as nomads. Most came as free men and some came alone as slaves of others. Nagel would describe them to Jarro and he would explain who they were and where they come from if he could. Nagel had a natural curiosity about people or perhaps down deep inside he was still hoping somehow to find his real family. His friend Jarro was very knowledgeable about the traveling strangers of the then, known world. The two of them spent a lot of special time together. Nagel often went with him and helped him gather the reeds down by the river in order to make more sandals. Jarro was honest, kindhearted and just a neat guy that liked you and he didn't care if you were a Nobody with no one to belong to. He just happened to be blind.

One day Nagel was doing his usual work at the Armen place and it was time to feed and check on Rasha, (she is the beautiful Ocelot upstairs in the Mistress' bedroom). He entered the room as always and set down the food and water, but she wasn't in her usual place. He started searching the many places she usually hid. Then he saw her! She was in the corner of the room crouched and ready to spring at something. "Rotten coconuts," It was his dog, little helpless Scrappy! He had followed Nagel up the stairs and was bounding into the room. Her eyes were fastened on the prey and her back leg muscles bunched and quivered ready to spring. Nagel screamed at her. Was it too late, would he see his helpless puppy torn up before his eyes? Then he remembered his magic whistle. It was tied to the waistband of his shirt. He grabbed it and blew hard. There was very little sound that he could hear but suddenly a pigeon flop landed on the window ledge. Rasha hated those birds! She tucked in her tail and retreated slowly under the bed. Wheee that was a close one! What would he do without that precious whistle? It had saved him on several occasions and he truly believed it had MAGIC and mystic powers. As he quickly gathered up his little fat puppy and darted out of the room, he thought back to the day he got the Magic Whistle.

⁂

"Come closer little boy, I have a gift for you." It was the crackling voice of a very old lady. "Don't be afraid," she continued. Earlier in the day he had seen her sitting beside the road on a blanket. The people who set her there had left her a goatskin bag filled with water, some dried fruit, and bread among other things. When Nagel looked at her, wispy white hair and thin bent body he wondered what her life had been like and what were the many memories locked in her mind... *When you were born, you cried and others rejoiced. Live your life so that when you die, others cry and you rejoice...* Time had made them very different from each other, at least in thoughts. He was looking ahead to his life and she was thinking back on hers. But she was lucky to have a family and know who she was, he thought to himself. And yet they both had the same physical human needs... *The thread of human emotions is the same in every age and race, and any century or time. To be loved, accepted, and even successful, burns in the heart of all of us...* Oh yes, it helps to belong somewhere.

Most of the time when loved ones are left behind, as this lady was, money and other valuable things were left also and that could be dangerous because others would rob them if they could. Sometimes families ran into hard times; lack of money, or a wagon broke down and so forth. It was sad but people who couldn't walk or ride any further got left behind to fare as best they could and that was usually not too good. But look at her, she is still smiling... *Living and dying is an art like everything else...*

The local street-boys saw her sitting there and they had made rude remarks and let the dogs bark at her. "Hey, whispered Nagel, I heard the candy man has leftover free candy today if you hurry over there"... *Whispered words can be more powerful then shouted petitions...* It was a little white lie but it worked. The boys wandered off and left her alone. Later in the day, when she saw him again, she held out her hand and beckoned for him to come near to her.

"I know you are a nice young man," she said softly, "and you tried to help me and I have a gift for you. My father gave it to me when I was a little girl. I have kept it all these years and I want you to have it." She stretched out a shaking, wrinkled hand, with the beautiful, shiny, SILVER whistle in her palm. Then she looked into his eyes and whispered, *"Don't let your past hold your future hostage"...* Here, TAKE it, I want you to have it! It came from a silversmith who lived and worked in the temple of Ur." Dropping her voice to a growl-like sound she continued,

"It has a special, sacred, Priestly blessing because IT IS MAGIC! It will help you all of your life! Don't EVER lose it." She pressed it into his hand and closed his fingers around it. And so it became his special treasure. He knew how to blow it when there was an emergency, you just blow in the hole on the top but he never figured out what all the other holes on it were used for and she hadn't explained exactly how the magic worked? He went back the next day to find her but she was gone.

Scrappy was growing up just fine and becoming a beautiful dog. He was stocky and strongly built like the usual country sheepdog, but with the softest gray fur and he still had a winsome adorable face.

"People just didn't understand dogs," Nagel said to himself. "Most of the time they couldn't even pet them right." He put his hand on Scrappys' head and using gentle, even pressure he stroked the length of his back several times. Then he did the same on his tummy, when he rolled over he scratched him a little under the chin. You had to think how it felt as if you were the dog. Some people just banged their hands up and down on a dog with no thought as to what it feels like to be the dog. He knew animals so well and he knew they were extremely sensitive and perceptive and they didn't judge you no matter where you came from or what you knew. Nagel had taught Scrappy to come, sit, stay, roll over and fetch a ball. He never left Nagels' side unless, of course, he was told to stay.

Master Armen seemed pleased with Nagels' work; things were going well and he was growing strong, tall, and healthy in spite of his unusual way of life. Then one day Master Gates told him. "Nagel take some food to the new slave upstairs." Nagel obliged and headed to the upper room with a basket of food that Mirna had fixed. This room had rows of polished mirrors and jars of perfume and costly oils and ceramic basins to wash your hair and so forth. It was where the women of the Armen Estate spent hours in pursuit of beauty... *A beautiful lady is an accident of nature. A beautiful old lady is a work of ART...* It was a special, very large room, for Women only. It was a place he seldom got to see. No men were allowed to enter. He hurried down the long hall enjoying the luscious scent coming from the basket and walked up to the very decoratively painted, arched entry door. He began looking all around for someone new.

Suddenly, he stopped and his eyes widened in amazement, there stood a man beside the entrance door the size of three men and he was black. The bulging muscles on his body were bigger then the exaggerated muscles on the statures of the godlike creatures in the fountain place. He was wearing a leather vest and a short loincloth and his fuzzy short hair was pure white. He had no other hair on his smooth, very dark skin. He stood there absolutely still, and if you could have painted him white, Nagel would have taken him for a beautiful new statue. Nagel froze right there in his steps and gave him a frightened stare. He just stared back. Nagel had never seen a black person up close and he threw down the basket of food and ran all the way back to the safety of Mirna's kitchen. He had just met Nio the eunuch, special guard for the Woman's Room. In time Nio would someday become a very special friend to him... *A true friend walks in when the rest of the world walks out...*

Nio

Wednesday came morning and he was free again to do as he pleased. Summer had turned to fall and he was a year older and maybe a bit wiser. They walked back to the hideout together a boy and his dog, a proven excellent combination from the beginning of time... *A dog teaches a boy, fidelity, perseverance, and to turn around three times before laying down...*

When he arrived and climbed up on the ledge it looked disturbed. Maybe someone had been up here? He checked and everything was there! Wait where was his leather pouch? It contained twenty-one glass beads and one silver shekel; it was the last part of the money he had. It was paid to him for feeding the burros whenever the leather trader was making deliveries on the south side of the city. Doubling up his long, lanky legs Nagel scooted down from the ledge of his hideout and went to look for his good friend Jarro. But he was not in his usual workshop spot beside the candy maker. Candy was usually a grasshopper or dried fruit on a skewer dipped in palm tree sugar.

He asked the candy man in a careful and polite manner, "Where was Jarro?" Nobody seemed to listen to a worried boy's questions! They were all talking about the group of men who had roughly seized and escorted Jarro away. Negal felt overwhelmed and helpless. He never realized how much he cared about and needed Jarro. What had happened and what could he do? He put the pieces of the stories together and realized what must have occurred. Jarro had been asked to make some very special shoes for a high-ranking officials' lady. When she came to get them and realized he was blind, she paid him with a Mite instead of a Shekel. A coin of a lesser value and she thought he wouldn't notice it... *He that would steal a pin would steal an ox...*

He shouted out in objection, "I may be blind but I am not dumb!" It was a little too loud. She refused the shoes and told her husband he had tried to cheat her.

"Where did they take Jarro and what did they do to him?" He thought of the DARK Street and a shiver ran through him. Nagel ran down by the canal and watched the reed cargo boats being pushed towards the river by men with long poles. One by one they floated by. Why didn't the street people stand up for Jarro? He couldn't think straight. He stared at the water in deep reflection. He remembered a time when no one would stand up for a little boy.

Chapter Five

The men fleeing down the river had roughly thrown the little boy in the back of the boat with a group of newly captured slaves. Some were injured and many were yelling out hysterically, still hoping to escape. The men had not yet had time to put chains on their feet and yokes on their necks, so they were guarding them with spears and swords. While all this went on the little boy scooted into the back corner of the boat and began crying. As the new slaves were placed one by one in the hold part of the boat, things calmed down and some order was restored. Then the sailor rogues began cleaning up the deck around him. Because he was so young and had a cut on his back they just put some chains on his ankles and left him there over night and into the next day. But he would not stop crying. In fact it got louder and louder as he realized what was happening to him.

He wanted his mother and father. He wanted so much to go home! They shouted SHUT UP- SHUT UP! He didn't understand the language. It would not have mattered anyway because he was frantically sobbing. Then one man grabbed him roughly and held him over the deep, cold rivers water and told him to SHUT UP or he would throw him in, chains and all. He stopped with a sudden gasp. From that time until now Nagel never cried again! Even if whipped or hurt he never cried but he also never laughed out loud. When you are a Nobody, from nowhere, it is better to be still, and stay out of the way.

He spent the rest of his free time moving his hideout to a more secluded place along the wall, closer to the reeds and willows at the waters edge. Now, Scrappy could climb up or down all by himself. He worked hard to make everything secure and keep his mind off of Jarro. That night he listened to the music of the street people, a flute and later a lute. It sounded slow and sad; everyone missed Jarro, but no one more than he. It was late, and almost dark, when he climbed into the new hideout place. The palm trees were silhouettes against the purple sky and he could hear wild animals calling off in the far distance somewhere across the flowing river. As he crawled into his bed and lay down, he never felt more like a helpless, alone Nobody. The magic whistle could not fix his problems this time. Neither Marmoset nor Scrappy could comfort him tonight. Still he would not let himself cry! *A day of sorrow is longer then a month of joy.*

He got back to the Armen place early on Saturday morning and started to lift and haul the large ceramic jars. The work seemed extra hard and Mirna noticed his sadder than usual face. At mid-day she stopped him in the hall and gave him a long, hard look. He blurted out his feelings and concern for his friend Jarro and told her what had happened. He knew he had to try and find him even if it meant running away again. She made him promise not to do anything so foolish but wait until Wednesday morning because she had a plan to help him. The next three days dragged by slowly. Nagel could hear Mirna working in the kitchen later then usual on Tuesday night.

Early the next morning, she said "Nagel come with me!" It was Mirna she was dressed extra nicely and she had an especially pretty basket in her hand and it smelled wonderful. He dressed quickly and straightened his hair and told Scrappy to stay. She led him up the stairway and into the elegant, but official area, of Master Armen. The attending guards hardly noticed her and waved them both inside…*The deeper into the palace you go, the fewer the people, but the greater the influence…* Master Armen was waiting for them. Nagel remembered the last time he had been in this room and the same feelings of fear came flooding over him again. Could he really trust this tall, handsome dark haired man? Master beckoned him to approach and he did, just as he had been trained to do, kneeling as respectfully as he could with his arms crossed on his chest. But then he slowly raised his head and stood up tall and secretly told his knees not to tremble. He needed to look Master straight in the eyes because he really had something important to say.

"Nagel you have worked hard and you have kept your PROMISE to me and if you have a problem I want to know about it," Master stated in a loud voice. Nagel forgot his fear and the whole story of his blind friend Jarro came rushing out in a tangle of twisted, sorrowful words. He added how loved and respected Jarro was and how hard he worked to make a living. Jarro was not just a blind beggar and he was not a Nobody.

Nagel continued, "I promise you Sire, on my honor, I will never, never run away again and I will work for you as long as I live, if Master Armen will somehow find my friend Jarro and bring him back alive!"

"Nagel I promise you I will give it a real try! I think I can, and if I can, I will!" Much to his surprise, Master even smiled at him a little. Then he turned and gave some orders to the man standing behind him. The guard received Mirnas' gift of skillfully prepared food and they were escorted out.

Sometimes boys feel thankful but they don't know what to say or do. Mirna just returned to the kitchen as usual and got real busy. Nagel was so thankful that she had taken the time to try and help him, he wanted to kiss her, but he didn't remember ever showing affection to anyone and didn't quite know how, so he kept quiet as usual. He called Scrappy and left for his hideout in the city of Nippur. Now he had to wait and see if he could trust Master Armen to keep his PROMISE!

It was late in the day when Nagel and Scrappy got back to the hideout. He ran the last block anxious to see if Jarro might be back. Noooo he wasn't!

He liked the new spot he had chosen for his hideout. It was closer to the street people and from this spot he could see Jarro's empty workbench. That way he would know if and when he came back. No one seemed to miss Jarro as much as he or maybe they just didn't want to talk about it. He also found his missing leather pouch and all the things were still in it. It was right there all along, hidden under some extra clothes. Early the next morning as he was still lying in his hideout bed, he heard loud, excited voices and shouting coming from the street people below him.

"Whoa, stop right here!" Amazingly some of the guards of the King had stopped in the streets below. The white and gold horse drawn chariot was a sight to see! It was pulled by two elegant matching blacks. Yeahhhh! They had JARRO! The guards very politely and kindly led him to his workbench. Not only was the full payment for the shoes given to him in silver coins, but he also received a bunch of orders for more new shoes.

"Happy Horned toads," Nagel was overjoyed and thankful to Master Armen! He had kept his promise even to a slave boy like himself. That had to be what had happened. Nagel felt strangely taller and more important inside, but he didn't mention his talk with Master Armen to anyone. He, Nagel, had made a real difference in the life of his best friend. He still wanted to do something extra special for Mirna. He didn't know how to thank her. The street people seemed very surprised that Jarro, a blind street person, had been freed from the Kings Palace prison and able to come back home. It was something not likely to ever happen again!

Nagel and some of the other street children ran up to check out the beautiful, matching horses that were effortlessly pulling the chariot. The guards shoed them out of the way and gave a clicking sound and off trotted the horses almost spinning the chariot wheels behind them. Nagel really liked horses. He knew Master Armen owned and raised hundreds of them. He enjoyed working with them and some day he hoped to have one of his very own… *He couldn't possibly have known how important this knowledge would become in his future…*

Jarro didn't have much to say about the whole incident. The weather was cooler changing into fall and some large fish had been spotted at the river. Nagel and several of the other children spent most of the day throwing rocks and sticks at them and they caught several large ones. The street people built a fire again that night and all shared a wonderful barbeque fish dinner. There were music and loud talking, and best of all, more story telling. It was a very pleasant evening, almost like having a family. But Jarro was very quiet and seemed extra tired so no one dared to ask him any questions about the incident, and they never knew what Nagel had done to help him get back home.

Chapter Six

Shopping in Nippur was a special thing. You could purchase nearly any thing from grain to nuts. People would travel up or down on the Euphrates River from miles around to see the nice selection of things, especially, the lovely woven fabrics. One dark, cloudy morning a group of travelers passed through the marketplace as Nagel was helping the pottery man. He was helping the venders get ready for the day as he usually did in order to earn his breakfast. He noticed one tall pretty woman looking at him rather closely. This lady even pointed him out to her fellow travelers and they began to talk among themselves while watching him. CRACK, a bit of thunder, FLASH, as lightening brightened up the dark morning sky! Then there was a sudden downpour, everyone ran for cover. The streets were quickly filled with splashing rain and mud puddles, and whenever things settled down, he didn't see her anymore. She had been dressed in white.

Later on that day when he asked Jarro about it: Jarro told him, "From your description, Nagel, it sounds like the people who live several miles down River at Big Bend, you can usually spot them in a crowd because they were taller and fairer then most folks around here in Nippur and Big Bend is famous for its white linen."

It was Saturday morning back at Armen place. Nagel did his work in good time and finished early. He still wanted to do something extra nice for Mirna. She said the apples were ripe along the back wall and she would very much like a bunch of them. So he took several baskets and started out there thinking he would surprise her with a bunch of big red apples. But on his way he passed by the metal shop and saw a small group of men working. It was Nio the new, huge, black slave. He was being taught how to heat the forge and make horseshoes, fix the wagon wheels, and so forth. Nagel and Scrappy paused to watch them pounding on the red-hot iron. Neo's dark skin was shining with drops of sweat. The sounds echoed out like a loud ringing TING- PING- TING- PING. It was almost like music. The hammers looked like they were dancing as they hit along the red, glowing metal bars.

"Jumping grasshoppers," The fire sparks were spraying up in the air! Nagel stood back transfixed by the sight. The men were shouting instruction at Nio but he didn't seem to understand what they wanted him to do. Nagel remembered how it was one day long ago when he couldn't understand the language.

❦

When the rogue sailors poled their reed boat into the port city of Uzz it was full of newly acquired slaves. Nagel was by far the youngest of them. He heard a lot of people speaking in strange languages with many words that he couldn't understand. He remembered feeling weak and sick; also the wound on his back was hurting painfully. He had been left lying on the deck with the chains on his ankles and not much food or water. While the prisoners were all lined up to be inspected like a bunch of animals to be sold, he just sat quietly on a large box of stolen goods and watched as the others were passed off to the highest bidders. It was a tall, loud, rough looking Gates doing most of the bidding and looking to purchase some of the stolen bounty and other goods as well. This was a common occurrence along the waterfront docks and no one questioned where the merchandise came from. After all the selections were made the new slaves still in chains would be lined up to walk the long, usually hot, dusty road to their new owner's place. Maybe they would overlook a little boy sitting quietly by himself. But Gates noticed him sitting there and asked the sailors how much for the little kid? After a few words and one small coin he was handed up onto one of the loaded donkey carts and off to the Armen Estate they went.

❦

Back to picking apples: Nagel and Scrappy found some of the apple trees growing along the back wall. He managed to pull down a few small, wormy apples and put them in the basket; but the real big red ones were growing on the rock wall toward the backside of the hill with several bushy branches resting high up over the top ledge. He found a rope- ladder in the brush at the base of the wall. He threw it up again and again until finally it hooked on top and he managed to climb up very carefully. The basket and his sandals were left at the bottom of the wall; he teetered along the top of the rough wall barefooted. As he glanced down he was surprised how high up it was, he felt a little sick to his stomach, it was soooo…. high. No one could have survived a fall from up here… *Slow scary music right here…* He bravely continued over to the overhanging branches heavy with big apples. Placing his bare feet one by one very carefully, he planned to pick off and drop a few of the apples down onto the sand around the basket below. He inched along until he reached the first of the overhanging branches where the biggest apples were and discovered something completely unexpected. There were big dark buzzing flies and something stunk.

"Leaping Lizards," There was a small goat carcass laying up there half eaten! He crawled along the top of the wall to get a closer look at it. ROAR! SNAP! GROWL! A large male lion had been lying in the shadows, hiding along the top of the wall under the very branch he was reaching for. It sprang right toward him, then turned and bounded up into the apple tree behind the wall and disappeared. Nagel screamed and jumped back. Wildly waving his arms he made a desperate attempt to catch his balance! But over the edge he went. It was too late! He was going DOWN, backward headfirst! Would it be painful to die? He had wanted to learn so many things, and find out who he really was; he was just too young to go like this. There was no time to blow the Silver Whistle. He closed his eyes tight and waited for the pain. Oh falling--down--down--down falling-

-faallliinngg! Then a strong black arm caught his head and shoulders and another one grabbed him behind his knees. It was big Nio! He had reached up and caught the falling boy as he came screaming down toward the bottom of the wall. Then down they tumbled in a pile together.

Nio had been looking for some more straw and fire chips for the Forge and had wandered over to right below the wall. There he found the empty basket, shoes, and Scrappy sitting there and he had anticipated what might be about to happen. His quick action had saved Nagel's life! Nio's back had taken the force of the falling weight of both of them as they smacked against some rocks; but except for a few scratches, they were all right. They laid there a moment in wonder of what had just happened. Then Nagel just stared at him in amazement a SECOND TIME! Again Nio just stared back. Nagel caught his breath and his mouth dropped open but he didn't know what to say. THANK YOU didn't seem like enough; now he wanted to do something REALLY special for two special people, Mirna and Nio!

Lions were very common around Nippur especially in the brush and trees along the rivers and canals. They were a smaller type of lion than their cousin the African lion that we are familiar with, but looked a lot the same otherwise. They usually did not attack people. They were very aggressive to get the sheep and goats especially in the spring when they were lambing. The spirit of the animals in the cat family was especially sacred and had to be honored by giving an offering in the temple if one was killed. The successful hunters was also honored and considered very brave.

No apples for Mirna, not tonight anyway. Master Armen was planning a HUNTING PARTY for early the next morning. Nagel was surprised how excited all the men of the household became when they heard about the lion and Nagel's close call. They quickly planned all the details for a hunt. The dogs would be trackers and trail the lion and the men would ride the horses they had worked so hard to train. The weapons would be bows and arrows and metal tipped spears about four feet long that Nio had been putting together. It would be a real test of their skill, equipment and the horses. They WELCOMED the challenge. He heard loud talking and the commotion of gathering up all the needed things. It continued until late into the night. Master Armen's son Ahan began to follow his father around begging to see if he could go along.

"No, you are too young and inexperienced in these things," he was told. "It would be just the men and boys who were skilled in riding and hunting." Nagel was tired and sore from his fall so he and, of course, Scrappy with him, retired early to his bed on the floor in the back of Mirna's kitchen. He was in for a big surprise. The next morning Nagel felt a hand roughly shaking him awake.

"What, what is it Master Gates?" He muttered. It was still dark, what was going on?

"Hurry and get up Nagel you are going on the hunt, with the rest of us! It is because of YOU we are going. Get on some clothes to travel in. You will have to ride a horse and carry a bow and arrow." Nagel fumbled around in the dim light for his favorite white tunic and pants.

"Where, where were those sandals? What about my dog and how, how long will we be gone," he asked, rubbing his still sleepy eyes and thinking do I really want to do this?

"Scrappy is going too, we need all the dogs to help us track the lion and we will be gone as long as it takes to get rid of it. If we don't he will come back and bring others with him," said an impatient Master Gates.

Chapter Seven

Twenty or more armed and mounted men and older boys were ready to ride out through the big wooden gates. Master Gates didn't wait for Nagel to mount up he just lifted him up overhead and dropped him onto the rough cloth and leather saddle and stuck the reins of the bridle in his hand. Erron the gatekeeper unlocked the heavy metal latch and the big wooden gates swung wide open. The little brown mare between his legs was very much awake and Nagel had to hang on. The dogs, including Scrappy, were barking and circling the riders in excitement. Down the palm-tree-lined lane they started, stepping along in a brisk walk. Master Armen was out front in the lead. Nagel didn't know it but after this hunting trip his life would NEVER be the same.

Nagel reined his little brown mare in behind the big speckled roan that Master Gates was mounted on. He was fully awake now, and his heart pounded with the realization of being a part of a surging gang of heavily armed, traveling men. Clip, clop, whinny, bark, with weapons held high and banners of the Armen family waving, they were a sight to behold and they knew it. People turned to stare as they rode through the streets of Nippur and along the canal and over some low wooden bridges. The sound of many horse hooves echoed loudly across the water. Oh, he wished that Jarro and the other street people could see him now! See him, Jarro couldn't see him, he was blind, but when he got back he would tell Jarro about every detail of this trip.

They rode on along the river's sandy banks with dust spraying up behind them. They squished through the marsh pools where the water was a frigid contrast to the morning spring air. Then on into the low trees and brush country, hoping the dogs would intercept the trail of the lion. Soon the city was almost out of sight, and looking out ahead of them, there was just open country and the wide shining river… *Grand flowing adventures type music here please…*

By now the sun was fully up and sparkled like fractured crystals across the water warming his face. His little mare stepped out in a steady beat, with a swing to her hips; the breeze tossed her long mane against his face. He had ridden a horse only a few times in his life and then only in the horse pen enclosure to assist the horse trainers. He felt the powerful muscles in her shoulders rise and fall as her hard round hoofs dug into the sand. He was glad the gods had created horses, or did they?

"I wonder how fast she can go and if I could stay on," he thought to himself. He watched how the other riders moved in a relaxed rhythm to the horse's naturally swinging motion and he tried to imitate them. He felt proud, grown-up and happy. He swallowed hard to keep his emotions from bubbling over too much, not real manly you know. Master Armen looked great on horseback. He rode a stocky well-trained black stallion, with a smooth stride to him. Nagel had never seen him in battledress. He had a leather helmet and vest with the Armen family symbol carved into it. The colors were red and blue with matching feathers woven into the design. His leggings were leather and the brilliantly colored blanket under his simple saddle was finely made, hand woven with great skill. He carried a spear and there was a curved wooden bow stretched across his strong broad shoulders and at least a dozen sharp arrows in his finely tooled leather quiver. Right behind him, and to one side, rode his heavily muscled new black slave Nio, who also looked rather formidable on the largest buckskin gelding Negal had ever seen…. *We need majestic French horns playing here.* Three hours later, he was tired, it was hot and his long sweaty legs were rubbing painfully along the mare's sides. *Stop the music*

"Maybe she was too fat for him, Nagel thought? How do you stop, why didn't they take a break"? Nagel could see they were approaching a small stream up ahead. Just then he heard a shout.

"Hold it up!" yelled Master Armen, "Water your horses, check the saddles and packs, tie down your weapons and get ready to RIDE!" The dogs had found a scent and were yelping, barking and circling. Nagel dismounted, or rather slipped off by his-self onto the sand, and found that his legs were a bit shaky and hard to control.

"How do you take a big horse through the sand and mud down a steep bank to the water with all the other horses and not get trampled to death, Nagel asked himself?" But he bravely tried it anyway and managed to follow along with the others and walk to one side, and the mare did the rest. If you are going to ride with the men you can't ask for help all the time, he thought. He cupped his hands and got a big drink for himself as well. He was learning a lot on this day.

They snacked on figs, goat cheese and dried meat; and he slipped some to Scrappy before remounting the mare. There was no trail to follow now, just the dog tracks spreading out ahead of them. They had bunched up into a tight group and were traveling fast trotting along and then they swung into a slow canter. Nagel was glad he wasn't carrying a weapon because he was very busy trying to stay on. He told himself to lean forward, hang onto the mane, stay in the middle and keep balanced. It was O.K! He was doing all right. The dogs had spotted something up ahead of them. They were barking and yelping louder and louder! The horses were running faster and faster. Nagel could feel his heart pounding along with their thundering hooves and he could feel the heat rising from the little brown mare's laboring body. After several miles of traveling through grasslands, desert and low hills they found several of the dogs circling a small tree, the other dogs were chasing something on up ahead.

Then someone shouted "THERE IT IS, THERE IT IS!" A large growling, snapping male lion was crouched in the top branches of one of the trees. The dogs were called back and several of the riders circled with bows drawn and ready. When it was all over, Master Armen fired the final arrow to make sure the lion was dead. There was a big racket of shouting and barking then they all dismounted and gathered to examine the kill. Maybe it was the same lion and maybe not? Nio was told to load the trophy lion up onto one of the packhorses, but the animal panicked, snorted and broke away from him, and then it ran up on a little hill behind a group of trees and vanished out of their sight. They decided to skin the lion right there.

"Where was Scrappy, thought a worried Nagel?" It was late into the afternoon. The tree shadows reached across the sandy hills like fingers on a man's hand. They had traveled way too far to return home before dark. The group would need to get settled right here before the sun began to set and they could find the runaway packhorse in the morning. "We need to unload and get ready for the night." Gates loudly announced. They didn't know it yet but this long day wasn't over and the real excitement was just beginning.

There was no water nearby, the horses and dogs would have to wait until they could find some in the morning. Some of the men had water in their goatskin bags and that would do for all of them for one night. They unsaddled and hobbled the horses. There was enough dry grass for them to graze on during the night. The blankets and saddle pads were spread out in a circle to be used for sleeping. Then they cleverly placed several pieces of rough horsehair rope in a big circle around the sleeping area. This would stop most creepy, crawling, creatures. Poisonous snakes and scorpions and such would be out in the warm desert sand tonight and usually the rope trick would stop them. They didn't like to slither over rough, sharp things. A light dinner was shared around a small fire. After talking over the days adventures awhile, they watched a brilliantly glowing sunset fade into darkness. Then they settled down for the night. Nagel was surprised how well he had ridden and how much he was accepted as one of the guys. He didn't feel like a slave boy or a Nobody tonight. It felt so good to lie down with Scrappy close by and relax a tired, dirty, and a bit sore body. There was a little light toward the East where the moon was just peeking up. The night was growing dark, cool and quiet.

LISTEN! LOOK! Wait a minute! What was that string of firelights coming down the hill? "Somebody is coming!" One of the men yelled out loudly! They were all up in a flash with hearts pounding. Who could be out here in this lonesome wilderness? Was it friend or foe? The dogs barked and the horses were alert and everyone jumped to their feet to stare at the strange approaching long path of torch-lights. There was no time to mount up or find your weapons; besides the group parading toward them greatly outnumbered their small bunch. Many things raced though Master Armen's mind. Had he gone too far into an enemy's territory? These men were approaching on foot. Did they want the horses? Were they armed? His little group backed into to a smaller and smaller bunch almost back to back and stood there with no one saying anything. They had not planned on ANYTHING like this!

The heavily armed line of men marched forward into the light of the fire a little too fast for comfort. When they stood around in the glow of the firelight, Nagel could see long, bushy hair on their heads and mostly animal skin clothing topped with tall leather boots. They carried axes and long sharp spears and held several big, shaggy, barking dogs on braided ropes. There was an odd smell about them and ALL the dogs were going crazy with barking.

…Some drums beating loudly would be appropriate here…

After much shouting to quiet the dogs including their own, the man in charge spoke out loud and clear! Master Armen's group all stood there dumfounded. No one knew what was being said, it was a different language that no one seemed to understand. The short, stocky leader came closer and loudly repeated the same words again and then again. Master Armen stepped forward and they glared at each other closely, face to face. It was a long tense moment and then Nio came forward. As he stepped into the light of the fire, the strange intruders all jumped back a few steps and a gasp was heard, followed by loud murmuring. Most of them had not in their lifetime, seen a black man and never a man so large and powerfully built as this. NIO KNEW THE LANGUAGE AND WHAT THEY WERE SAYING! At least he knew just enough to understand the message. That is after a lot of repeating and haggling and waving of hands.

Nio told master Armen. "They want to know what we were doing here and who we are?" Then the strangers were shown the dead lion skin and carcass and heard where they were from and how the group had come to be here. After much talking among themselves, surprisingly they held out their hands in welcome signs, saying come, come! It was plain the small group was to follow the strangers. There wasn't much choice. It was a demand! All the things were quickly gathered up and horses and dogs were collected and they made ready to go.

"Jumping kangaroo rats, thought Nagel!" What was going to happen to us and where was this strange army of smelly, funny dressed men taking us and why?" He called for Scrappy to stay close by his side. After grabbing up his things and quickly pulling his sandals back on, he caught the little brown mare. His fingers were shaking so badly it was hard to unfasten her hobbles. Then leading her behind him, he started slowly following along with the rest of the little group. He was thankful for the now brightly shining moonlight. If he lived through all this, it would be an adventure to remember!

They all marched up the hill, bunched closely together with their feet sinking ankle deep into the sand. Some of the strange, smelly intruders were behind them and some ahead of them. They were following the same trail where the runaway packhorse had snorted off to. Then a little further on up over the top of the ridge and SMACK-O, nothing could have prepared them for such a magnificent sight.

… *Loud grand flowing big country music here please…*

"IT WAS AN OASIS!" It was all green and lush with trees and grass and a large body of water in the center. It stretched out as far as they could see in the moonlight. Spread out below them were hundreds of sparkling campfires and large tents scattered along the mirror-like shimmering water. As they continued on, walking along in wide-eyed astonishment, following the intruders along a well-worn path, they could see and hear large herds of sheep, goats and Asses in the pastures and lush meadows on both sides of them. Date- palm trees, along with willow, bamboo, many kinds of fruit trees, and plants in abundance were shining in the dim light. But the most surprising and frightening thing of all was a large group of people; men, women and children, shouting loudly and parading out to meet them.

Chapter Eight

OASIS: Fertile tract of land that occurs in a desert wherever a permanent supply of fresh water is available. It can be two acres or a vast area. The underground water source may be as far away as 500 miles. The water travels through underground sandstone aquifers. Often they are laid out like an uneven string of pearls across a vast wilderness.

Nagel could hardly believe his eyes. He had never seen or heard of an Oasis. If only Jarro were here, maybe he could explain what was happening. These people seemed friendly, too friendly. They were grabbing the horses and petting the dogs and staring at the small group of men. A wildly curious gang surrounded Nio, but nobody dared to touch him.

It was mass confusion! After what seemed like forever the short heavyset leader, named Lugan, yelled at the group surrounding them, and everyone stepped back and became quiet. Through Nio, he told Master Armen, that he and his small of group men were to stay here for tonight and maybe longer? The HORSES would be put in a corral with water, lots of grass and be safely guarded and watched throughout the night. There was a large tent for all of the men. They would be escorted to it. They obliged King Lugan and followed the men in charge along the trail to the tent, still carrying their weapons with them and whispering among themselves what to do? It was one of the biggest, squarest looking tents Nagel had ever seen. He glanced around inside and saw it was made from many animal hides skillfully sewn together and beautifully decorated with paint (plant dyes) and brightly colored feathers. Indeed there were all kinds of foods spread out on blanketed tables in the back of the tent. Fruits, cheeses, dried meat, bread, plus wine and milk and so many more things, some of the likes of which Nagel had never seen.

"Well, they haven't killed us yet, and they are willing to FEED us, just maybe we could survive this," thought Nagel. He found himself edging closer and closer to the food and soon he was into it. Most of the Armen group was a bit too nervous to enjoy all the bountiful things spread before them. When they were inside and seated in the large tent, King Lugan politely but firmly, asked for all the weapons to be handed over. The men did so very begrudgingly with long sideway glances at each other. They were told they must stay here in the tent. What was going on here? It was past midnight by now, and the camp outside was getting quiet. The dogs would have to sleep outside the tent door. Later in the night Scrappy snuck into lie beside Nagel. King Lugan's armed men surrounded and guarded the tent during the rest of the loooong night.

MORNING AT THE OASIS (SETCA)… When Nagel awoke, Scrappy was outside the tent snooping around and checking out the strange dogs and everything new to him. Master Armen and most of the men were already having a loud and lively conference under the shade of the Palm trees. There were wooden benches, chairs and tables but most of the men were sitting on the ground. As Nagel causally walked out to join them he noticed several groups of children of all ages intently watching him. One of the little boys pointed at his Silver Whistle. He quickly tucked it under his white tunic. Again there was plenty of food and drink but not many were eating. They were just noisily all trying to talk at once. Of course Nio was in the middle interpreting as best he could but it appeared they were all going to be prisoners of these strange people.

As most of the bizarre looking people were milling around watching the little group, they continued checking out the men's weapons, clothes, sandals, and anything else they had. But more then anything they were crowding around the HORSES.

These people were originally from the plains of Shinar and spoke Arkakian. They were nomadic-roaming herdsmen that had settled here around this string of Oasis's about 200 years ago. King Lugan was "Your Majesty King Lugan the third." It was a dynasty that he ruled with an iron hand. The three largest Oases had an overall population of about 3,000 people or more. This Oasis, where the King usually resided was called Setca which means; water of life in Arkakian. These slowly flowing lakes were doted like precious jewels set in the otherwise rather dry barren countryside covering an area of perhaps a total of 50 miles or more. These nomadic people moved the herds and flock from one Oasis to the other. They went wherever the best grazing was at the time. There were chickens, ducks, and geese, with herds of sheep and goats. They had a few camels, herds of Asses (there were wild Jackasses in the hillsides). But they had No HORSES! They were helpless against roaming and raiding bands of horsemen that had attacked and killed many of them in the years past. Sometimes these people were friendly to strangers and sometimes not. Master Armen knew if they wanted something they would just take it. But so far, and for some strange reason they were being treated like welcome guests.

WE WANT TO GO HOME

Day-one
"Your Majesty King Lugan, you have been most generous and kind to us but we must go home now," said Master Armen. He presented King Lugan with the only things he could find

to give him. A gift of the still bloody lion skin and a beautiful bow, complete with a quiver and arrows, as he bowed graciously. It had been left tied to his saddle and missed when the weapons were confiscated. These were very nice weapons which were unfamiliar to these people. They passed them all around and examined them with great care and curiosity. They had axes and spears but had never learned to use a bow and arrows. There was a lot of excited murmuring at the sight of the fresh Lion skin.

Suddenly King Lugan grabbed the weapons, roughly pushed them away, and stood up shouting, "I already HAVE you and ALL your things and I do not need more of your gifts. I need HORSES!" But later he gathered up all of the gifts with a little smile on his face. What was he thinking?

King Hugan the third, of Setca

Oh that was it, they wanted the horses! Later that night, Master Armen had a plan. "We have three stallions and nineteen mares and we need them all to get home. We must convince King Lugan that we will bring him horses, lots of horses, if he lets us go." Their tent was being heavily guarded every night and they felt closely watched during the day as well. They talked and figured what to do until it was nearly morning. The next day they asked for another conference with the king and his nomadic people. But King Lugan would not meet with them.

These people lived in a beautiful place and they loved to show it off. There was a white, sandy beach sloping down to the water and then on the far side high rising clay and sandstone banks with rough holes in it. Sometimes crocodiles and vipers were seen over there. "Stay away from there they were warned!" These were considered sacred and they didn't disturb them if possible. That is why most everyone wore boots in the tall grass and Nagel learned why they all smelled so strange. There were mosquitoes and knats in abundance. The people rubbed special oil on each other. It came from the seed of the San San Weed which the children gathered in the marsh. It was a natural repellent. The knats could get in your hair, and the bites were so bad it could make your head swell painfully. There were all kinds of strange bugs, lizards, frogs, poisonous and non-poisonous snakes and several kinds of fish. Deer, Antelope, gazelles, burros and wild pigs were common off and on as well as the lions and wild dogs. It was a good life and easy living but only if you knew all of the tricks.

The acres of tall, grassy pasturelands were spread out like a green blanket over the rolling hills and dotted with many different kinds of trees, fragrant plants, and beautiful butterflies decorating the abundant colorful flowers. The warm air was filled with the songs of many kinds of strange birds and you could hear the ducks and geese calling from the lake. Nagel took it all in with continuing amazement! If ever there were a real paradise, Setca was it!

WE WANT TO GO HOME

Day-two

"King Lugan, sir if you will be so kind as to return our weapons and horses we promise to go home and then we will return with many gifts and more horses for you and your men." The King laughed and slapped his leg and said. "I will NOT let you take the horses; and as for you, if you return at all you will return to your home riding on Jackasses!" Then he hit his fist on the arm of the chair for emphasis. Oh things were not looking too good. What to do, thought Master Armen?

THAT NIGHT WAS LIKE A WILD, CRAZY PARTY! They built a large bonfire on the sandy beach and served all kinds of wonderful food. There were whole roasted goats, pigs roasted with yams in their mouths, and colorful fruit and vegetables of all kinds. Nagel loved the coconut milk and date bread. King Lugan was served first and then the Armen group were served and treated just as royally. After all had feasted and drank their fill, the food was taken away and the REAL FUN began! Drums, flutes, small mandolins, tambourines, gourd shakers, rattle sticks, and a few more music makers, made the night loud and lively. Add the dancers, dressed in colorful and flowing garments with feathered headdresses, then throw in great singers, storytellers and play actors.

"Tell us the Lion story again they yelled, tell us how the little boy fell off the high wall and the black man caught him when the lion attacked." Tell us how you rode horses through the desert countryside and shot the lion out of the tree!" By the light of the fire they told it again and again embellishing it a bit as they went. Then the play actors got into it and began to act it out. One man ran out and got the real lion skin and put it over his head and he would prance around acting like he was a lion, with a snap, growl, and clawing the air. One of the little boys would jump backward, scream and make believe he was falling (off a chair) when the dancing lion jumped at him.

This was repeated several times all with MUCH knee-slapping laughter. This was their main form of entertainment and they loved it. After more food and drink, even Gates and the small group got into it before the night was over. They would prance around in a circle and act like riders searching the desert for the lion, and when they saw it (the man covered in the lion skin) they would chase him. After much shouting waving and pointing, they made believe they were shooting the bow and arrow at him. He would fall down after thrashing about awhile then he rolled over with his feet in the air, and become the dead lion, all to more and more laughter. Then they asked Nagel to play the part of the boy falling off the wall, because they all knew it had really happened to him. From that time on he became known as, "THE LION BOY."

WE WANT TO GO HOME

Day-three

"King Lugan, sir, you and your men will not be able to just jump on these fine horses and ride them like a Jackass. It will take a long time to train you to be able to ride them. You need us, we can teach you how. We have several expert horsemen here with us. You can become the best riders in this part of the world," coxed Master Armen.

"We now have stallions and mares and we can raise all the horses we need, replied King Lugan." In almost a growl he continued, "And we will learn to ride without your help one way or another, so why would we really need any of YOU!"

The next beautiful day was spent exploring the Oasis of Setca, and checking out the strange type of colorful chickens, sheep and goats. Things went very slowly because of the communication problem. Nio couldn't understand all of what was said that well either. They drew pictures in the sand and gestured a lot. These people had made fascinating waxed animal skin canoes that were waterproof and skimmed over the lake with ease. They had learned to use the natural material around them quite well. There was a special pole and palm frond building (The lodge) in the center of the village. It was just for men only with King Lugan presiding and officiating over most everything. They met there for special priestly and religious ceremonies and all meetings of importance.

WE WANT TO GO HOME

Day-four

"King Lugan sir, you cannot turn these fine horses loose with all the wild jackasses around here; they will breed with the mares and you will have a bunch of mules and mules cannot reproduce anything," spoke up Master Armen. The Kings answer was, "We will think about that for a day or so. Meanwhile here is something you are going to need!" The men were asked to remove their sandals and then they were all given oiled lambskin boots with beautiful stitching and different fascinating designs on them. Nagel, THE LION BOY, received a special WHITE pair.

Nagel was beginning to spend his time in making friends with many of the children, and he taught them several games including how to play the game, Makeme. They didn't seem to know he was just a Nobody. He could learn to like this place! These beautiful, tan, healthy people appeared to be a happy, friendly bunch with the girls and women a little shy and more to the quiet side. But Master Armen noticed his men were still not given back their weapons and the horses were being very closely guarded. After another day, the Armen group became even more restless, and in spite of the wonderful hospitality, they wanted to start home. Some of them wanted to fight and overpower these people and force their way home. They began to question the leadership and ability of Master Armen, who felt without their weapons and horses it could be the death of all them. Could he keep them together and stay in control? He asked to speak to King Lugan again.

WE WANT TO GO HOME

Day-five

"All right we need you, declared King Lugan, so you will start early tomorrow morning and teach us all we need to know about horses."

"Begging your pardon sir but what happens after we teach your men and boys all about horses, questioned Master Armen?"

Throwing his head back and slapping his leg again. "We will ride that horse when we catch it, now won't we Masser Armenee" shouted, laughing King Lugan!

They had bought some time and maybe it would save their lives, could they teach these strange nomadic men to train and ride horses? Remember there is a language problem, or was it just a different dialogue, because if you really listened to them you could understand some of it? It remained to be seen.

We Need Horses

Chapter Nine

"Where were the lion hunters?" The Master Armen household was becoming alarmed! The men should have returned days ago. Without Master Armen, Gates, Nio, and our hero Nagel, and the others the place was not functioning very well. "How can we send out a search party if no one knows which way they went?" said Mirna, wringing her hands in concern. It was decided to send a message of alarm to the King of Nippur who was a personal friend of Master Armen. Someone must go and search for them!

Jarro, (Nagels special blind friend) had noticed his little pal did not come on Wednesday morning as usual. He checked with the Candyman and others and no one had seen Nagel, not even the street children. His hideout was empty. Only Marmoset the little monkey came and went by herself. If Nagel didn't return soon Jarro decided he himself would find his way to Master Armen's palace and ask about him. They needed to know he was missing! Jarro wanted someone to FIND NAGEL!

As for Nagel it was a wonderful time. He had no heavy jars to haul and no one to boss him around. The children all liked him and he enjoyed the food and the evening story telling was terrific. He was the "THE LION BOY," running around in his special white boots. When it was hot they went swimming down by the beautiful sandy beach. They were free to paddle the canoes and explore the whole area as long as they spent some time guarding the sheep and goats. There was some water hauling and dung chips and wood to get for the fire and he helped to do the work along with all the other children. But they spent long days in wonderful play and he and Scrappy loved it. He made special friends with several of the children. In fact he was beginning to smile and even laugh a bit in spite of himself. But he did miss Jarro and wondered if he would ever see him again?

There was one girl he really enjoyed being with. She was about his age and could run as fast as he. They couldn't talk of things past or future because they didn't understand each other but there was hand waving and looking and pointing at the things around them and a lot of just laughing together. He asked her name?

"Zalakkene," she shyly replied. There followed a long moment of silence. "May I call you Sara" he asked? She just smiled and so it was "Sara".

LEARNING ABOUT HORSES

TRAINING --DAY ONE….All about horses: When approaching a strange horse walk up to his shoulder. Do not look directly in his eye. He considers that a challenge to him. If he wheels to run from you, keep clear of his back end. It is his natural impulse to kick out as he runs away from you. If one horse starts to run, the others often panic and try to run also. Horses are very sensitive and respond well to gentle repetitions when being trained. You must teach him to respect you. We will show you more on that later. They practiced catching and leading the horses around and just getting acquainted as to handling them.

Sara

TRAINING--DAY TWO....Food, feet and the best horse to ride: A male horse is called a stallion-(when young, a colt) the female is called a mare-(when young, a filly) A gelding is a castrated male.

Stallion – strong, smart, determined, but may go bonkers around a breeding mare and can be dangerous. Mare – very smart, strong instincts, very alert but moody. Gelding – the best ride, loyal, strong dependable, willing to go.

Things to know: Their favorite food is green grass but they can live on hay and grain. They eat several hours of the day and need food and clean water at least twice a day and maybe more. A good horse has good feet. Large and round is the best shape to have. Rocks and sharp things must be cleaned out of the hoof, as needed. Shoes are optional and needed only on rough and rocky ground. How to pick up the feet: He cannot lift his foot if he is standing on it. So when lifting a front foot lean your shoulder into his and unbalance him onto the opposite foot, or turn his head away from the side you are picking up. The hind feet can best be reached by running your hand from the hip slowly down to the foot and pulling it slightly forward as you raise it. He needs to be brushed and cleaned before riding. You cannot pet or brush him too much. He loves it. They all practiced picking up the horse's feet and cleaning them.

TRAINING--DAY THREE...What he can do: A good horse can run 30 to 35 miles an hour with you on it, if you stay balanced and not interfere with the action. If he is in good condition he can travel over a hundred miles in one day. Saddle marks, white spots on the back near the shoulders are not natural. It is a poorly fitting saddle and a misplaced blanket that causes it. The saddle fits on the backside of the withers. (Shoulder bone) The girth strap that holds the saddle in place should be snug but not so tight that you can't get two fingers under it. This strap lies a few inches behind the front legs. Horses are by nature gregarious animals but they can live alone if needed. His teeth continue to grow throughout his lifetime. Twenty to thirty-five years is the average lifespan. They practiced putting on the blankets, headpieces and learned how to saddle up properly.

A good horse can be taught to make a sliding stop on a coin and turn like a swinging gate. He is controlled by the reins, the balance of your weight, and pressure of your legs, feet, and your voice.

TRAINING--DAY-FOUR...How he thinks: He has a very strong sense of smell and hearing. The sense of sight is his least trusted thing. He does not see the world the way you do. He cannot see well up close or straight ahead and each of his eyes works independently from the other and so the training must be repeated on each side. Waving your hands or some object close around his head, ears, and eyes are very annoying to him. His greatest power and defense is to run away and so he has a fear of being caught in something, such as a rope, mud hole, vines or something that will trap his feet. Light and dark shadows on the ground or water where he cannot see the bottom are all a terror to him and he must be trained to accept them. High jumps are possible but not natural and must be taught to him, because of his poor vision. Because horses are gregarious and follow a leader, if you really want a well-trained horse you must earn his respect and become that leader for him.

A round corral of poles and ropes was to be constructed. It would be about 60 feet in diameter. Master Gates drew out a pattern for them to follow. The corral would be needed in the learning how to ride faze of the program.

⁂

Meanwhile the children played, Roll the Bones, while setting in the shade of the big tent: shake them in a cup and roll out on a blanket and do as many tricks that the pattern of bones counted out. They were having fun. When they were tired of that they ran out in the pastureland with the dogs and checked the sheep and goats and brought in some wood for tonight's fire, as they had been told to do. They had plans for the next morning.

Let's take some food with us and go exploring along the lake in the canoes. We can take some spears and chase pig, they decided. Nagel was so excited about going he had a hard time sleeping that night.

The next morning, Nagel, Scrappy, and Sara all got into one canoe. And several of the other children got into four or five of the other canoes. They all paddled out across the lake. The deep, dark water was as smooth as a polished stone…. *Flowing light smooth water music here….*They did find and chase some pigs. The dogs ran after the rabbits, deer, and whatever else they could find. After the children swam and played in the lake they drew pictures in the sand, and then decided to make a fort along the bank behind the trees. They cut down some poles and cleared a spot and soon they had a nice little shelter started. "We will come back tomorrow and finish it."

But the next morning; "Nagel, you can not go with the kids today!" Demanded a rather agitated Master Gates, "You have to help us teach and train these men how to ride, we must do this so we can find a way to get back home!"

Because he was light in weight and agile he was chosen to be the rider. The little brown mare was the horse being used to demonstrate how to ride. This was the part these nomadic people had been waiting for. How to ride! He did not consider himself to be an excellent rider but the hunting trip had helped him improve a little. He had worked with the trainers several times before at Master Armen's place just doing what they asked. He remembered seeing experienced riders gracefully swing up onto their horses in one smooth motion not even using the stirrups. He and the mare were already standing at the side of the training arena. The whole village had gathered around to watch this final demonstration. He grabbed a hold of her mane, then without a hand from anyone, he swung his right leg up and pushed hard with the left… *Don't show-off too much here Nagel!*

"Crazy crickets," he made it. He almost slides too far up over her withers but the trainer, steadied him a little. He hoped no one noticed that part. He moved the mare with a squeeze of his legs to the center of the round corral, and while sitting tall, he collected the reins and… waited for instructions. He had worked with this trainer (Chad) before and he pretty much knew what was wanted. "All right Nagel, have the mare step out into a brisk walk first, make a few circles around the ring and then show us a slow trot for several turns," stated Chad. He knew he should keep his hands low by her withers and maintaining a soft rein.

"Stay balanced in the center of her and no bouncing," he told himself quietly. Horse and rider traveled smoothly in a continuous circle around the outer edge but still inside the ring. He was doing just fine, but then he noticed SARA was in the crowd watching him! She was standing by King Lugan. Why was she was always sitting or standing beside Him? He thought to himself. Why hadn't Sara gone with the kids across the lake to finish building the fort? There she stood and she was watching HIM intently. Was that admiration shining in her eyes? Whoa, he almost ran over the trainer. Chad had to jump out of the way. Now they wanted him to show the mare at a canter? (A canter is a slow floating like gallop.) ... *Brisk rhythmic riding music here, if you will please...*

Somebody help me or blow my Magic Whistle for me, he thought to himself. But he gracefully and smoothly moved the mare into a canter like a pro, and then it suddenly dawned on him... SARA was a princess, SHE WAS KING LUGANS DAUGHTER! The little brown mare floated gracefully around in a canter she even took the proper lead, as Nagel rocked slowly in rhythm with her. Then he turned and cantered the other direction again in the proper lead. The demonstration continued for several hours... *Note; when in a gallop a horse has to be in the right lead when turning right and the left lead when turning left. He does this automatically when running loose but when being ridden the rider must clue him before the turn, because he does not know ahead of time which way you are going asked him to go.*

"OK Nagel, now let's show them what she can really do!" commanded the trainer, Chad. They all stood back and swung the gate open wide for him. He walked the mare out while still sitting balanced and tall, all the time he was talking to her in a soft but exciting voice that only she could hear. He loosely collected the reins then all at the same time he suddenly relaxed them, quickly leaned forward, and squeezed his legs a bit and then let her go wide open. She KNEW what he wanted! *Wildly beating drums would be nice here*

Horse and rider raced wildly up a small hill near by. Bits of dirt flew out behind them as the little brown mare's sharp hoofs dug into the ground; very swiftly she continued to gain speed as she raced up to the top of the hill. Then when he sat down deeper into the saddle and tightened the reins she came to a smooth sliding stop, as Nagel skillfully leaned a bit to the right and pressed her left side with his left leg she collected her powerful back leg muscles and wheeled completely around to the right. They thundered back as fast as they could go. They finished with another graceful sliding stop right in front of the crowd of wide-eyed, nearly astonished, Setca people. Her head was in a balanced position, the reins were loose and he had STAYED ON! It was a very exciting moment and they all hollered and cheered, Yehh! Yaa! Hurrah! Here's to The Lion Boy and his wonderful racing horse! This was what they had been waiting to see, the speed, power, and glory of a HORSE! The demonstration was over. (Just maybe Nagel knew more than he thought about horses.)

The little Brown mare

The Black Stallion

The little brown mare was breathing hard. She stood quietly right where he had stopped her but she trembled a bit when they all cheered. She had done everything he had asked of her. Nagel unsaddled and walked the mare until she was dry, then he brushed her quite a while and fed her well. She was a good mare and he softly told her so again and again. The entire Oasis of Setca was filled with a wild celebration all that evening and late into the night. But Nagel was quite sore and tired right now, he had used a few muscles he didn't know he had. He and Scrappy retired to the big tent early, but not before hearing Master Armen say. "Thank you Nagel I am very proud of you, you did very well today." …*The craving to be appreciated is one of the deepest principles of Human Nature…*

Nagel was gaining new respect for Master's calm, decisive leadership, which was not an easy task with rough, crochity, King Lugan and his own restless men. … *Keep your fears to yourself but share your courage with others…*

Chapter Ten

The next morning: Master Armen asked to speak to King Lugan again.

"Good day to you, your majesty," he began. "I am sure we can come to some kind of an agreement today because my men and I are leaving for home tomorrow morning. We have taught you the basics and completed a brief overview of what it will take for you and your men to be great horsemen and now I need to go and get your horses for you," he directly and flatly stated. He was greeted with a long, thoughtful, silent stare and then…

"Come with me Master Armen, into my private sanctuary (for men only) and we will talk about what will happen tomorrow!" This was the special large hide covered lodge-like building which he had never been invited to enter. Master Armen felt very powerless and apprehensive. Maybe this was good, maybe NOT… It is a mistake to look too far ahead only one chain in the link of destiny can be handled at a time…

First there was a hand washing ritual and some lying out of special rugs by the king's servants. Then they were seated inside the lodge and served a sweet yellow drink. Soon the talks began between just the two of them! After several hours of heated discussion they sent for Nio to be an exact interpreter and make sure they understood each other. But later that afternoon a nervous Master Gates went out alone and asked to speak privately to King Lugan.

THE AGREEMENT

King Lugan laid out what his demands would be. It was as follows:

At least forty fine trained horses, not just mares and colts. He would need two of the horses to be older stallions which were proven breeders.

He continued, "You MUST return within thirty days and you WILL come back because I will pay you well for them. My people will make our own saddles and bridles by using one of yours for a pattern. You will take FOUR of my men along with you. They will ride Asses, so you will have to go slow. I will pay you in fine leather boots, wool blankets, woven fabrics of your choice, and oh yes, I have GOLD. You will receive one pair of boots, two blankets or fabrics, and one shekel of gold, for each horse that I accept. They must be trained to ride and in excellent condition. You will bring NO strangers back with you! I will keep your best black stallion and one mare, and last but not least, I will keep TWO of your men as hostages and they will remain here at Setca until you return! It will be any two men that I choose!"

Master Armen replied, "But Your Majesty, what if I refuse your offer or what happens if I can't make it back in time?"

King Lugan: "You will NOT refuse my offer because first of all I am willing to pay you in GOLD, and second, remember I already have your horses right now and I don't really need you or your men! We have sacred crocodiles that get ravenously hungry. I hope you understand my meaning! Thirty days is plenty of time and if you don't come back on time, I will be very angry and pity the two men left behind!"

"Could you show me the GOLD?" asked Master Armen.

"Could you show me all the HORSES?" loudly shouted King Lugan, with irritation in his voice, while he pounded his fist on the arm of the chair.

"Will you give us back our weapons before we go?" asked Master Armen.

"Yes" yelled the King.

"I will go and talk this over with my men and then give you an answer?" said, Master Armen.

"NO! You will agree or disagree right now and you WILL keep your word" loudly stated the King! There was a long moment of silence as Master Armen's mind began racing to imagine all the things that might go wrong.

"YES, I will AGREE!" said Master Armen. What else could he do? They each put their own signature mark on a piece of sheepskin and the King counted out thirty eight small marbles and two larger marbles for the older Stallions. One marble was for each horse to be delivered. They wrapped and tied up the sheepskin into a bundle with the marbles inside it. The bundle was then securely tied up in the almost sacred LION skin. The two leaders stood up face to face with a long look at each other, then both bowed stiffly and the contract was made.

WOW, at long last they could go home! The men were overjoyed and elated. They swung each other in circles and Nagel grabbed Scrappy by the front paws and danced around with him. The equipment was made ready, gathered up, and dusted off. The horses were fed extra grain and the water bags were filled and so forth. They were all homesick and anxious to go.

Suddenly they stopped getting ready and one of them said. "Wait a minute, who are the two guys that will be LEFT behind?" Nagel felt sad that two men would have to stay behind almost like prisoners. He wondered who it would be. However it was only for thirty days, that is, if everything went all right. There had been so many good times here. He thought about the many friends he had made and he would miss them, especially, Sara. He needed some time to tell her goodbye but right now he wanted to get ready to go home. It was the first time in his life he was glad to be just a Nobody slave boy, so of course they would not want to keep him.

"The King will tell us tonight who he has picked to stay here after our final dinner with them," said Master Armen.

After dinner the Setca people wanted to playact THE LION BOY story again. But the King Lugan said NO, because he had an announcement to make. Everyone got quiet and Master Armen's men stood at attention nervously looking at each other.

Please play a soft drum roll here.

"All of our guests, their horses, dogs, and weapons will be leaving in the morning, except for two men who will stay with us!" loudly stated King Lugan. The whole group groaned in disappointment. They had enjoyed their guests. He continued. "We will also keep the big black stallion and the little brown mare. Very soon the threat of invading armed horsemen will no longer be a problem for our people!" Yeah, a cheer sounded at that statement. He continued, "The two men are going to stay here until the others return in thirty days with forty horses! Which two will be the hostages? I have chosen NIO and NAGEL, to stay here!" With a crocked little smile he added, "They will continue to be our guests."

Big black Nio just stared blankly into space, just as if he had already known he would be one of the chosen ones, but Nagel's mouth dropped open in surprise. "There, there, must be some mistake! But, Master Armen," he stammered, and with real pleading in his eyes he said, "I- I- cannot stay here, Mirna needs me and I have to check on Jarro and Marmoset. I just can't STAY here!" There was a long look but no answer from Master Armen.

Early the next morning; the men saddled up the horses, gathered up their weapons and things and left right after a rather dark and cloudy sunrise. They went rather quietly compared to the morning they had started out on the lion hunt. Even the dogs just circled and whined before leaving. Their clothes were dirty and worn looking, as were their faces. The four men appointed to go with them from Setca, mounted on the Asses, went first to get a head start. As Master Armen rode out he looked at Nio and nodding his head toward Nagel, he said, "Nio, take good care of him, he is a good boy!" Then he squeezed his horse and soon they were ALL GONE! Then Nagel felt like he was NOBODY from nowhere, as he watched until they all rode out of sight. The black stallion and the little brown mare in the corral continued to whinny and run back and forth all that day in protest of being left behind.

Chapter Eleven

The two hostages were assigned a much smaller tent. The first thing Nagel did was to find a red piece of clay and put a mark on the inside of the tent for DAY ONE. Of course Scrappy chose to stay with his master. They were watched during the day and guarded very closely at night. But they were still allowed do as they pleased most of the time during the day, even while being watched.

That night Nagel dreamed of the white feathers again.

It seemed like the fun times were over. Everyone had their own work to do. The children were moving the sheep and goats to another and better grazing place. Most of the women were busy making rugs, boots, fabrics, and doing the usual gathering of food for all the others. The men set out to make saddles and bridles like the ones they had seen. Sara was helping her mother spin wool and dye it in all different colors and hanging it up to dry.

Several days later: "H-e-l-l-o baby, H-e-l-l-o baby," Nagel whispered in a weak voice. He was holding baby Benny out at arms length. At least he had a diaper on thought Nagel. What to do? Sarah had said to TALK to him. He had often talked to Scrappy when no one was listening. Nagel had NEVER held a baby or even been very close to one, and to be honest, he was scared to death of them because he did not understand them at all.

Early this morning he had asked, "Where is Sarah?" When the children of Setca had gathered to play for the day she was not there with them, "Oh, she is going to baby sit her little cousin Ben," said one of them. How awful, thought Nagel.

"Poor Sarah," he said out loud.

"Oh no she loves to do it," they all said at once. Really that was hard to believe when he thought how HE felt about BABIES. She is at her aunt's place down there by that large cottonwood tree; they pointed the direction out to him. Nagel found her sitting on a blanket holding the baby. Typical baby, he was crying. "Sara would you please come in here a minute," called her aunt. Sarah jumped up and handed the baby to Nagel and left. She just reached out and put IT in his arms.

EEEOOOUUWW!! There he stood holding a crying baby. "Here talk to him, his name is Benny, and I will be right back in a few minutes," she had said, while plopping the baby into his arms. Nagel would rather hold a baby crocodile. Then Nagel looked into his sad little crying face, and after a few moments, he held him a bit closer and started to talk to him. He was surprised how good he smelled and, "Happy horned toads," he even quite crying and…soon they had him smiling and giggling out loud as they played peek-a-boo and let him look at all the fascinating things that were so new to him. You guessed it Sarah and Nagel had a great morning playing with little Benny. Nagel had a complete change of attitude about babies. One learns truth though the heart not the intellect or understanding.

Nio had become involved with helping to mend and repair the canoes. They had to be dried out and rewaxed to be in good working order and stay afloat. But sliding one of them up onto the repair ramp took three strong men. Nio sat and watched them struggle for a while, and then he stepped forward, took hold of the rope and pulled a large canoe up easily and gracefully all by himself. The men just laughed and joked about it. Then some of the other strong guys tried to do it also, but they couldn't do it as easily as Nio. It soon became a kind of manly fun competition thing. He liked to be helpful, so the Setca men took advantage of it and enjoyed having him there. Nagel and Scrappy spent a lot of time down by the lake exploring the deeper holes where the bigger fish lurked. He was learning to fish by using the net on the long poles like the Setca people used. Whenever he had time to be by himself he began thinking about Big Bend, the town that Jarro had said the woman in the pretty white dress might be from; the woman who had stared at him so oddly just before the rainstorm in Nippur. Did she know him? Anyway somebody must remember the little boy that was kidnapped. Of course there were many other people taken that tragic day.

Then one day King Lugan asked Nagel to come and talk to him.

"Nagel," he began, "I would like my daughter Zalakkene (Sara) to learn to ride a horse and since we have two horses here and you are an expert horseman, would you be willing to show her a little more about horses?"

"Yes sir, King Lugan, I would be glad to do that," replied Nagel. It was set up for the following morning and so the private lessons began. The language was beginning to be less and less of a problem because so many words were just pronounced a little differently, and if you really listened, you could understand almost all of what was said.

They started out by just brushing and leading the horses here and there, and then Nagel helped Sara up onto the little brown mare and showed her some of the basics. Things like how to start, turn, and stop maneuvers. She was very quick to learn and soon he climbed on the black stallion and off they went. At first he led the mare along side of him, but soon she learned how to use the reins and was doing quite well. Wow, this was a job he liked. He felt that he was not really an expert horseman but what could he do if everyone assumed he knew all about it. He actually was hoping this big, black, powerful stallion would not challenge him too much because he wasn't to sure what to do if he did.

They both couldn't wait to go riding every morning. It was a wonderful place to explore and she knew her way all over the countryside. They didn't bother with the saddles; they just jumped on bareback, using the smooth slide up and on in one move method, which they both mastered quite well. Every day was a fun adventure for them. They would ride along side by side with Scrappy running ahead and then behind a while, laughing and talking about everything in the world as they went along. Then Nagel got a SHOCK! She was surprised to learn he was a slave-boy, because Master Gates had told the king that he was Master Armen's own SON! They decided to keep it a secret because her father would be very angry and think he had been deceived if he knew Nagel was just a slave-boy.

Sara, Nagel, and Scrappy

"Oh, funny fat frogs! That is why King Lugan chose him to stay behind as one of the hostages! The King thought that Master Armen would never leave his own son here in Setca and not come back for him," thought Nagel to himself. Master Armen's son, "They thought he was master Armen's own son." He wished inside that somehow it would become true, and then he would finally belong somewhere and to someone. What about Sara would it make a difference to her if she knew he was just a Nobody? He tried to explain his life and how he lived in two places as best as he could but he doubted that she could really understand all of it. In fact he didn't either, to be honest. He told her about Marmoset, his pet monkey, and his special friend Jarro being like a father to him. No wait, he was perhaps more like a grandfather. He knew that Sara being raised a princess as she had been, was so completely different than his rough past. Sometimes they stopped and let the horses graze if the grass was extra green and tall.

On one occasion she asked about the Magic Whistle that he kept with him all the time. He told her about the poor old lady, how he got it, and all of the times it had helped him with the magic powers in it. She thought it was very pretty and tried to blow it with no luck, and then she stuck a piece of cork in the end and he was pleasantly surprised. By fingering the different holes on the side she could play a tune. He taught her the song about "Sweet Sara" and even sang it to her. She played along on the Magic Whistle which she had turned into a kind of short flute.

Down in some green valley in a lonesome place where the wild birds do whistle and their notes do increase, Farwell pretty Sara I bid you adieu but I dream of pretty Sara wherever I go.

Sometimes they went swimming if it was really hot. They even rode the horses into the lake just for fun. They had hours and hours of good times together.

Master Armen and his entourage arrived home in two and a half days without any problem. His friends and neighbors were so excited he had returned

safely. They wanted to hear all of the wild adventure stories of the strange people living in a beautiful land; the lion hunt was almost forgotten. King Lugan had insisted that the guests return with the lion skin so there was something to show for the hunt.

Mirna was extremely upset that Nagel had been left behind, but she realized they had very little choice in the matter. When the stories reached Master Armen's friend, King Tukuli of Nippur, things almost got out of hand. The King wanted to collect his army and wipe out the whole bunch of Setca people. In lieu of how his friends had been forced to stay there in Setca against their will and the two hostages were still being held captive and treated like prisoners.

"I understand how you feel my dear friend, but you must remember, they will pay us well for the horses and the two slaves are very special. Nio is a most unusual slave and very useful to me, and Nagel is becoming more like a son then a slave-boy. I really don't want anything to happen to ether one of them," said Master Armen.

When he told the King about the payments of beautiful boots as well as cloth and GOLD, they began to plan how and where to collect the horses for the return trip.

"Gates, I want to send someone to check on Jarro and tell him where Nagel is," said Master Armen. "I told Nagel I would do that." Gates arranged for that to be done. Jarro was understandably very upset at the news, and said Master Armen should not have taken Nagel out there in the first place.

⤝⤞

"Oh Nio, you should have seen what Sara did today, for a girl she is the best swimmer I have ever seen and she can ride almost as well as me already," said Nagel. "She said she never had so much fun in her life as when she is with me and and…"

"Nagel, if you don't quit talking about Sara I will have to plug my ears with sheep's wool," returned Nio. King Lugan saw what was happening and tried to keep Sara busy with a few other things now and then but she managed to slip away to be with Nagel again and again.

One day as they stopped to rest the horses, they were sitting under the shade of a big nut tree laughing as they cracked and ate the nuts together. Nagel suddenly realized how much he really cared for her. It seemed that his heart had broken loose and was floating up like a bird inside of him. She was like a beautiful wild creature, but he couldn't decide which one. When he really looked at her she was not quite a perfect beauty in face and figure, it was mostly the feeling of happiness she gave him that he enjoyed so much. He had never felt this way before. Let's face it, Nagel was absolutely TWITERPATED! He stared at her shinning brown hair and sparkling dark eyes and looked at the freckles on her nose and noticed the glow of softness along her neck and shoulders. Her skin was so smooth it almost looked like it had been powdered… *There are… four things that are too amazing for me, the way of an eagle in the sky, the way of a snake on a rock, the way of a ship on the high sea, and the way of a (young) man with a (young) maiden. Pro.30: 19*

She told him about a special place that she had always dreamed of exploring. It was an unusual outcropping of rocks up high on the tallest mountain several miles behind the lake. She was a little afraid to go there all by herself. He replied that because of the horses, if they started early they could probably get there in just a few hours, and he would take her there if she really wanted to go, maybe tomorrow they could go.

It was day twelve already. Nagel added the twelfth red mark on the inside of the tent. Nio and Nagel talked a lot of what to do if Master Armen was late. Nagel warned Sara again to please not tell the King he was really not Master Armens' son. She agreed it might be better for him that way. This was the day they were going to the mysterious mountains. It had rained the night before and the air was extra clean and everything seemed sooo fresh. Even the horses were fresh and eager to go, as was Scrappy as usual. They let them travel at a gallop for a while, just rocking with the rhythm and the wonderful sense of controlling such a strong fast animal between your legs, almost like you were that animal and the power was coming from inside your own body. *How about some exciting traveling music here?*

When they finally slowed down, most of the trees and grassland were fading out behind them. The thought that he could just keep going and escape occurred to Nagel but he had no water bag and how could he leave Nio alone to such a horrible fate. He had seen the hot temper of King Lugan before, besides he didn't know which direction to go from this side of the mountains.

The increasingly steep incline ahead was mostly barren sandstone and rock. So agile and sure-footed was the little brown mare she pushed on ahead of the big, black stallion and Sara laughed and called out, "Women rule!" Soon the horses could climb no higher. They would have to go on foot the rest of the way up to the top. When hobbles were laced on, the horses were left to graze in a spot of dry grass. Nagel and Sara began the hard climbing part, using their hands to pull themselves along for well over an hour and soon the top was in sight. Sara stopped to look all around several times. Nagel could see this was a very special thing for her.

When they got to the very last highest rocks where the view all around them was unbelievably beautiful, Sara climbed up onto the top alone. *Let's play some beautiful flowing grand scene music now and feel a soft warm wind blowing….*

She stood on the ledge of the highest point and became very quiet as if in deep thought. It was as if she were up there all by herself. Then she leaned into the wind with her long dark hair blowing out behind her and held out her arms as if she were flying and sang softly to herself. The lovely haunting melody seemed to float down over the whole valley beneath them. It was several minutes before she climbed back down.

"Oh NOW I know what kind of wild creature she is like," thought Nagel to himself as he watched her, "she is a beautiful butterfly getting ready to fly, starting to spiral up into the air." And suddenly more then anything else HE wanted to be like a warm breeze beneath her wings!

King Lugan was becoming increasingly nervous and upset as the appointed DAY drew near. One time he overheard some of the children talking, and someone mentioned that Nagel was just a slave-boy. When he found out it was really true he raged about it for days. He said it made him look like a fool to make that serious of a mistake to assume that sneaky Master Gates told the truth when he said Nagel was Master Armen's son. It could jeopardize the whole agreement! He ordered some of his men to build a strong cage, large enough to hold two men as prisoners inside. They also made some wooden stocks that could fasten your head and hands in through the bars. One was for an extra large person? If things went wrong, the King was going to have the last word. The Setca people began to look at Nio and Nagel in a strange way. Was it fear or sympathy, or did they knew what the King might do?

The two hostages, Neo and Nagel figured they could be in serious trouble. What if master Armen was late or didn't come at all, they knew they were just expendable slaves. After several long secret talks in the middle of the night they decided they absolutely MUST escape the day before the due DAY, in case things went wrong.

"If we could just get to the horses they could never stop us," said Nagel. They made a detailed plan of how they might get away on the horses and called that plan # One. That might go wrong because they knew the horses were being guarded so closely, but then so was their own little tent. They would also have a back-up plan # Two, escape by canoe. And what if King Lugan put them in that wooden cage for safekeeping? Then there was no plan that could help them!

"Nagel I would have to have an extra large canoe to stay afloat," said Nio. He had another very IMPORTANT reason for not wanting to escape by plan #Two, but he didn't want to tell Nagel what it was.

The time passed quickly and soon Nagel marked in red the twenty-fifth[th] day. About that same time in Nippur, Master Armen was sending word throughout the near countryside looking for a few extra horses. Most everyone had a few mares and colts and breeding stock but there were very few prime three and four year old, already trained to be ridden horses. He planned on leaving on the twenty-seventh day just to make sure he was in Setca on time. He was taking along with him most of the same men from the Lion hunting party because King Lugan had said he must bring NO strangers. The four men from Setca were being treated as special guests but they preferred to camp out in the back field with their burros; however, they enjoyed Mirna's cooking very much.

On the twenty-seven[th] day, Master Armen started out with forty-four horses (four extra in case of any problems) plus what they were riding. Some of his men were not too eager to return to Setca. The weather had changed a little the day before but they were still well on their way when a strong wind came up and it quickly turned into a sandstorm. They collected the horses into a little valley and waited behind some trees to see if it would pass. It was a choking storm for man and beast and it was almost impossible to see where you were going.

"Let's wait it out or we might go the wrong way and get off our trail," he told the men.

Chapter Twelve

It was the evening of the Twenty-ninth day. Nagel marked it in red. Everyone was edgy and nervous. Would Master Armen come back and bring the horses? Nio and he had made a lot of different plans and still didn't know WHAT to do, but it would have to be now or never. Tomorrow was THE APPOINTED DAY! The people of Setca had built several corrals and made halters and leather goods, and were anxiously awaiting their horses. Nagel had informed Sara what he and Nio had planned, but she was not to help them at all because she would have to face her father, the King, if she did. He was really going to miss her and quietly told her goodbye that evening. She said very little, maybe she didn't believe him.

It was dark, late, and still, when they made their move. The two guards were as usual, standing just outside of their tent so…*Music full of suspense here please*

"Nagel, whispered Nio, climb up on my shoulders and take the knife." As quietly as he possibly could Nagel pulled himself up as Nio held him as high as he could reach and he quietly, slowly, cut a long slit in the top section of the tent. Then he reached up and got hold of the rope he had fastened up there secretly several days ago, it was securely tied to the limb of a big oak tree growing over the top of the tent. Nagel went first, slowly pulling himself up into the leafy branches and waited for Nio to do the same. They couldn't even whisper now, because the guards were too close and nearly beneath them. Climbing out onto the far branches and then dropping down to the ground took a several minutes or more because they had to go quietly and so carefully. What about Scrappy? What if he didn't follow them outside of the tent or if the guards saw him and stopped him? How could Nagel leave his precious dog behind?

The guards looked up into the trees a few times at the slight creaking sounds but said nothing to each other. Then the hostages were both down and into some nearby bushes when Scrappy decided to join them. Nagel held his breath but nobody paid any attention as the dog walked out of the tent and into the darkness. They slipped along a little brushy gully, inching toward the horse corral hoping the two guards might not be too alert tonight. When they saw the horses, it looked hopeless.

"Great Galloping Ghosts," thought Nagel. There were four of them, each with a tall, sharp spear, two by the back rail and two standing near the gate.

"Let's forget the horses and go with plan #Two. Let's get down to the water fast before they find out we are missing out of our tent," whispered Nagel.

"Try and find a canoe, a BIG one!" whispered Nio. The moon was already up a little just as it had been on that first night when they came here days and days ago, while on the Lion Hunt, but it was not quite light enough to see where the trail went! They kept bumping into things and each other. Oh no, one of the Setca dogs was starting to bark at them.

"Oh, may the gods help us! We must find the canoes, which WAY to go?" Suddenly a small, slim figure appeared out of the shadows near the water's edge and silently beckoned them to come this way. It was SARA! She had already launched a canoe and placed two paddles, a small axe, dried food in a bag, and a large goatskin bag of water in the bottom of the canoe. She also handed Nagel a small leather pouch which he silently stuck into one of his white boots. Sara steadied the craft as the two men and the dog climbed in slowly and quietly. Not a word was even whispered, but as Nagel slipped past her she reached her hand up behind his head and pulled him down to her and gently kissed him on the mouth.

OHEYHAWA!!! (*Silently in his head*) No one had ever done that to him! Not that he knew of anyway! He mind began racing.

"She kissed me! She kissed me! She kissed me!" Then the pounding of his heart told him that someday, if he lived through all this and the gods were willing, HE WOULD be back!

The windstorm had slowed Master Armen's group, they still arrived on the thirty[th] day, but it was late in the afternoon. King Lugan got his HORSES and Master Armen got his GOLD and so forth. The King was VERY pleased with the four extra horses.

Where were the HOSTAGES? No one knew except Sara and she wasn't saying anything! After a three-day search a very sad and disappointed Master Armen and his group left for home without Nio and Nagel! What would he tell Mirna and what to do about long waiting Jarro?

<hr>

The small canoe sat very deep into the water and when they stuck the paddles in and started to paddle, it made too much noise, so they used their hands to slowly and quietly paddle it along until they were about half way out into the lake. Nagel remembered where he and the children had gone to build the play fort and he headed that way. He thought he could find it even in the dark. As they neared the shore little rivulets of water were trickling over the low sides of the canoe faster and faster and more and more!

"Keep it steady and sit still!" loudly whispered Nio. His opened-wide eyes were filled with fear and shining like two white spots in his dark face. They both paddled faster and faster trying hard to keep the canoe afloat but the water just kept bubbling in as the canoe slowly filled up and sank, and went under. Scrappy did a dog paddle for the nearby shore and Nagel swam around and tried to gather up some of the things before they sank.

"Where was Nio? What is wrong with him?" He was splashing and thrashing around and going down under the water.

"Help, Help, Nagel I can't swim," he gasped in a whisper, while still trying to be quiet. Nagel immediately started to swim to him, NOOOO we would both drown if he grabs me, he thought, but I HALF to help him! What can I do? He spun around in the water and saw the goatskin water bag was still floating. He grabbed it and using one of the paddles pushed it toward sputtering and coughing Nio. He reached out and grabbed it but he pushed it too far under and was still struggling to keep his head up on top of the water! *Scary frantic suspenseful music here*

"Nio, don't panic! Calm down and keep your head down closer to the water. Hang on lightly and relax if you can!" It worked! Nio got a big breath; but he continued to yell as softly as he could, "Nagel help me, Nagel you must help me!"

Nagel managed to get a hold of the cord tied to the bag and slowly while swimming with all his might he towed Nio in toward the shore. They stumbled up on the bank together still trying to get their breath and fell in a pile. They laid there in the moonlight and stared at each other. Then suddenly Nio began to laugh. What is wrong with him? Has he gone crazy?

Then Nagel remembered something too and he began to laugh. They had done this before when Nagel had fallen off the high, rock wall and Nio had caught him and saved his life. They had laid there in a pile of rocks and stared at each other. Now the sandal was on the other foot and he had saved Nio's life. They lay there laughing softly together for quite a while. *Even in the most serious of times a little laughter is a good thing.* Now he knew why Nio didn't like the #Two, escape by canoe plan. Big tough, strong Nio could NOT even SWIM!

It was too dark and dangerous to travel through the grass and brush tonight. You had to cut through the vines and abundant foliage even to go a little way, plus the grass was full of snakes and other creepy things. In places this part of the shore was impassable even during the daylight when you could see where you were going. There was no need to worry about hiding the canoe. It had gone clear under. With luck they would not be missed until morning.

"Let's get in the fort," said Nagel. They found a sheepskin and some rags to lie on. It was left over from when the kids had been playing here. They sent Scrappy into the fort first to check it out for varmints. Then all three of them slept restlessly in the little shelter for awhile and got up and left as soon as it was light enough to see anything at all. When Nagel pulled his boots on, he remembered the leather pouch. It was all wet, but still there. He looked inside of it and there were three shiny gold coins. Sara had taken a real risk for them. May the gods bless her, what would they have done without the help of sweet Sara? He thought again of her kiss...

They had to make good time because they knew King Lugan would quickly send out the message of alarm that he was looking for two fugitives with a dog. *Traveling music alternating with feelings of suspense here please...* MOST WANTED: One extra large black man, one young boy along with a shaggy sheep dog!

They had lost the axe in the lake but they still had the knife, the kind of soggy bag of food and the water bag. Sara had carefully instructed them to go north to the next Oasis, buy some supplies and a burro and then head toward the west branch of the Tigress River and always travel upstream. From that point on, if they needed directions there were many boatpeople and travelers that could tell them how to get back to Nippur.

On foot it was about a three or four-day walk so be prepared. The plans they made while living in the tent had not included exactly where they would go after the escape, if they survived it, but Nagel had assumed they both wanted to return to Master Armen's place. Maybe he was WRONG?

◔◕◔◕◔◕◕◔

King Lugan was red-faced furious that they had escaped the night before the big day! He sent out runners to check all around the Oasis, but no luck. Then when Master Armen with all the men and horses finally arrived he turned his attention to his new horses and forgot about the two escaped fugitives. But Sara could not forget about Nagel. .She felt so empty and lonesome now that he was GONE. She had been completely happy before he came, so why would she be so sad and pine for him now? But she DID! "Will I ever see him again," She thought? They were much too young for strong feelings like LOVE or were they? Does love know an age limit? Sara's feelings were very real! *How about a sad lonely love song here?*

This next oasis was much smaller, with less people, then Setca. It had much more open, dry land. There were fields of grain with olive trees planted all around them with fruit and nut orchards along with beautiful vineyards. The people were more into farming then the Setca people had been. Nio and Nagel arrived tired, with torn and dirty clothes. There had been a nice trail between the two Oases' and they made good time after they once got out of the marshlands and swamps. They did not want to attract attention to themselves, but Nio was very hard to disguise. In fact many people stared openly at the three strangers, a pretty sheep dog, a tall, long haired young man, and a very BIG, black man. At times some of the town folks even followed behind the three strangers to get a closer look.

"Nagel, we need a spear or an ax, another bag for water, some light supplies of food and maybe some different clothes," said Nio.

"Lets see how far the money will take us and maybe we can even get a Jackass to pack the stuff for us and then we can travel much faster." There were several groups of venders in the heart of town with clothes, blankets, sandals, boots, food and so forth and so they went shopping. It was almost like the streets of Nippur, thought Nagel. However there was NOTHING big enough, in all of the clothes they searched through to fit Nio. One very wise, older lady gave them some grape juice, bread and chicken and told them to sit down, rest and eat. Then she cleverly began to fashion a colorful blanket into a vest and pants for Nio.

Wow, they hadn't realized how hungry they were and quickly ate and Nagel even asked for more. Scrappy gobbled up all of the leftovers. Nio noticed the man (the lady's husband) also had two Jackasses in a pen behind his shop-like tent. One was a big strong, husky one and the other, a little knock-kneed kind of skinny critter.

"How much for one of the pack animals," Nio asked?

"Well they were really not for sale," said the man. But when Nagel went to pay the woman for the clothes and her husband saw one of the GOLD coins, he quickly gathered up everything they had said they needed and put it in a pile for them.

And then he changed his mind, and said, "You can have the clothes, the weapons, the food and everything, along with one Jackass for THAT gold coin." But when they started to go, he could not bear to part with the big pretty Jack, so he threw in a packsaddle and extra grain to make up the difference and hauled out the skinny little Jackass. They gave him the gold coin, packed up everything and got ready as quickly as they could. They knew which way to go. It was the opposite direction from Master Armen's place. It would still be the smartest thing to do because, number one, no one would be looking for them this far north; and number two, they would eventually reach the Tigress River and maybe get a boat ride up to Ur. Then they could travel across land to the Euphrates River and on home to Nippur. Thanks to Sara they still had two gold coins.

They were very anxious to leave town but the little Jackass was NOT! Nagel tried pulling and pushing her and even twisting her tail, just anything to keep her going, but NOTHING worked. The expert horseman couldn't even move a little Jackass! It was red-faced embarrassing. He felt like everyone in town was watching them.

"The grain," said Nio "Let's get out the grain and feed her some of it and then hang a basket of it on a stick in front of her nose." They did. It worked! She shuffled right out following behind them and they headed down the trail. Soon all four of them were moving right along. The brightly colored blanket, custom made into clothes, fit Nio just fine. Nagel thought about his favorite white tunic, and sadly remembered that it had been left behind, torn and dirty in a pile. But now there was a new striped yellow and red shirt and pants that fit him just right. Scrappy took the lead while the two men walked side by side. The little knock-kneed Jackass, which they named "Boots" (because her two hind feet and ankles were white,) was following close behind. She looked even smaller with the saddle and fairly large pack tied on her back. She had a funny shuffling stride to her but she was surprisingly strong.

Had they truly escaped and could they make it home? How far would they go? Nio was a very private, rather quiet person and sometimes, like now, they walked along in silence.

They passed other travelers on the trail, some with herds of animals and others with just a few pack animals; many seemed to be in family groups. Most of them wanted to stop and talk to them but others kept to themselves... *Light hearted walking through the country music with doves and quail calling sounds here...*

Scrappy and Boots

Boots and Scrappy

It was always better to travel along with several in a bunch rather then just two because of the danger of bandits; they were out there and made a living taking advantage of the unwary traveler. There were many places to camp overnight along the trail. Some even had wells or places like a spring to get fresh water. They made good time and camped off the road a little ways at a water hole that first night.

The second day Nagel noticed Nio slowing down and looking off to the right toward the far mountains off and on all day. When they stopped for water and a food break there was a fork in the trail ahead of them, and it headed off to the right. Then Nio told him some very surprising news.

"Nagel I have to go home to MY family and that is not back at Master Armen's place. My home is over there, he pointed off to the distant hazy Blue Mountains. It is many, many miles northeast of here. You see, he continued, I have two sons and a daughter and a beautiful wife, or I did before I was taken away from them. I must return to them if I can possibly get there," he said almost softly to himself. Nagel was speechless; it took him completely by surprise, but of course why would Nio want go back to being a slave when he could be a FREE man. He never thought of Nio as having a wife and children. This was Nio's opportunity to GO HOME!

Then Nio looked right at him and said, "If you want to go back to Master Armen's place, I am sorry but from here on you will have to go on ALONE!"

Chapter Thirteen

Back in Nippur the news of the two hostages disappearing was heartbreaking to Jarro. All of the street people, who were friends of Nagel were very sad to hear he had not been found even after days of searching for him. As time went on, Master Armen made it a point to visit Jarro on occasion and order a few sandals from him as well. One day he invited him to come and live at the Armen's place. Jarro said he would consider it but only if he were needed there. Marmoset had taken up with the man who had the traveling animal show. *Chattering monkey noise and bird and animal sounds here please.* She was lonesome and had become fascinated with some young rabbits in a cage. So the man agreed with Jarro and the street people that he should take her with him when he left town. She was so cute and everybody loved watching her do summersaults and other tricks for a treat or some nuts. So she became a welcome part of his animal show.

Nagel, Scrappy, and Boots would continue on alone. Nio would take the trail to the right that led up over the mountains. They had strong feelings for each other and hated to part, and it took them a while to say goodbye. Two men of different races, from different worlds, who had both been slaves, they were very unlikely to have ever been friends to say the least. They had been thrown together for a time by strange circumstances and now they would part. They both knew no matter what happened they would never be together again as they had once been. They had a mutual respect for each other and a caring trusting relationship. As they hugged and wished each other to have a great life, Nagel whispered in his Nio's ear: "Would you please learn to swim!"

He laughed and said, "I am going to work on that!"

Before Nio left they drew sticks to see who got what of the supplies. Nio took the knife, the long spear, and one of the two remaining gold coins, plus they divided the food in half and he took the smaller water bag. He would need the coin to buy passage to sail west after he got to the big water (Persian Gulf). He told Nagel to try and find a group of people that was going the same way as he, and travel along with them. It would be much safer then to go on alone. He hoped to do the same himself. Nagel knew no one would ever bother Nio, not if they were in their right mind but he didn't say it.

Nagel got the burro, the small ax, the large water bag, one gold coin and the other half of the food. Nio did not look back, as he left. Nagel stood and watched until he was completely out of sight before he started out again.

Nagel (who has become a tall, lanky, teenager by now) and of course Scrappy and Boots were on their way and on their OWN. When he made that promise to Master Armen, to never run away again and to work for him as long as he lived if needed to help his friend Jarro, he meant it and he intended to keep his PROMISE!

He found some travelers and they visited with him for a while and then invited him to join up and go along with them but they turned off on another trail after a few hours. As he walked along with nothing but his thoughts, he realized there were still so many things for him to learn. A good teacher could tell him all about the many mysteries of life because he sure had questions to ask.

Of course he still wanted to find out about his family and where he had come from. He also could use some kind of skills to earn a living if he were ever going to be a free man… *Thoughtful deep thinking tunes here, then turning into suspenseful drum sounds…* But right NOW he could use some lessons in manly self-defense, because there were two shady characters approaching him from behind a group of trees, along the left side of the trail.

"Stop barking and growling Scrappy, what is the matter with you?" inquired Nagel.

"Where are you going boy?" asked the taller (ner-do-well) man. The darker shorter man slowly started circling behind them; he was checking out the burro and Nagel's weapons and supplies. The men were both in torn and very dirty clothes and had their hair tied up in back because it had not been cared for in a LONG time. They both carried long wide knives tucked into their belt. If these were travelers, where were their things or pack animals, thought Nagel? "Where are you going little boy?" the strange man repeated more loudly.

"Well ahhh I am on my way to join my friends' right up there on that hill," Nagel lied nervously. "It is a good thing that the gold coin is hidden away in my boot," he thought to himself.

"Why are you traveling alone and where did you get that pretty dog?" drawled the same man. Nagel didn't answer him. The other one continued slowly walking around behind him.

"Where is my ax and why did I pack it away?" Nagel silently asked himself. As they edged up even closer Scrappy broke into a fierce spell of snarling and barking. The taller man gave Nagel a funny smile and they both stopped, and then stepped back a bit.

Then the taller one looked at his partner and said, "Well, we have to be on our way so have a good trip kid and take care of that nice dog O.K?" Nagel wasted no time in pulling Boots into a fast trot and back onto the trail. He moved out as quickly as the three of them could go and scanned the horizon hoping to see some other travelers he could join up with. The trail ahead of them took a big sweeping turn around to the left. He just started to breathe a sigh of relief, when Scrappy began growling again.

"Dirty Lizards", he thought, I just saw something moving behind the rocks up there along the right side of the trail. What if those two creepy guys have taken a short-cut made a circle and hurried on ahead and were waiting for him to pass by?

If Nio were here they wouldn't bother with me, he thought. But Nio was NOT here and he had to figure out what to do on his own! Were they still behind me or on up ahead of me? He quickly whirled Boots around and ran back down the trail as fast as he could get her to go. Then the three of them turned sharply to the right and scurried up into a little gully and over some rocks and continued climbing up higher onto the side of the hill, trying to walk on the gravel and grass and not leave a trail that anyone could follow… *Fast, wildly beating drums here.. .*

They were hidden out of sight from the trail beneath and out of breath when they finally stopped and tucked themselves under some nearby bushes. Boots began to eat them, but at least she was quiet. He waited there for what seemed like hours but it looked like no one had followed them! Boots pulled away from him and climbed up further on the hillside, when he caught up with her she had found a little green spot of grass with a spring nearby and she was knee deep in the muddy water getting a drink for her self. It was late in the day and this would be a safe place to stay for the night, he hoped. It was already a little cold but he had the saddle blankets and of course Scrappy would help to keep him warm. He really wasn't afraid because he had been alone many times in the streets of Nippur. However this was a bit different because it was not in a city but up on a strange mountainside.

Before dark, he and Scrappy hiked around and explored the hillside behind the water spring and he noticed several places that looked like there might be a cave or two up on the rocks by the top of the mountain. He and the street boys had explored the caves in the hills at the end of the Dark Lane in Nippur. Caves were very exciting but you needed at least two-torch lights, in case one went out and left you in the dark, which of course, he didn't have any. He had heard scary stories of people who never came back after exploring caves. He also noticed some footprints and a slight trail here and there along the hill-side; however they seemed to be very old tracks.

But there were fresh wild Jackass hoof prints everywhere. "The animals probably came here for the green grass and water," he thought. He would have to keep a close watch on Boots in case she tried to escape and join up with the wild ones. He planned to stay right here tonight and not go back down to the road. It felt lonely already and he was thankful for the animals to give him some company. He put the hobbles on and removed the saddle and packs from the burro and set the blankets to dry out some. He sat on the side of the grassy hill, petting Scrappy awhile then ate part of the date cakes and some dried fish. He feed some left over to his dog and got a big drink from the water bag. He could refill it at the spring in the morning and Boots could have all the grass and water she wanted tonight; anyway that was one good thing about hiding up here.

Chapter Fourteen

The next day it was a beautiful morning!…*Glorious sunrise music here…* After breakfast and before he loaded up Boots, he and Scrappy went up to take another look at the caves, before leaving the hillside. When he ventured into the smaller cave, it became pitch black too fast and smelled like animals in there so they backed out. Then the "kid" side of him won out again and he decided to check out the larger one. It was real cool within a few feet of the entrance. He had heard caves stay the same temperature all year around no matter what the outside temperature is. It quickly became dark and cold inside and he had to step carefully and feel his way along. There was a pile of dirt and a few rocks they needed to climb over. He thought about turning around but then, what was that small ray of light up ahead? He really was curious to see what was in there? Maybe there was another entrance or another opening up there and he could go clear through and out the other side. That would be so neat! So he pressed on a little farther. He stopped to smell the air and just listen for a while. Then the HAIR on the back of his NECK stood up! Drums beating wildly here just like Nagel's heart! There was a moaning sound coming from somewhere inside of this cave!

He and the dog SCRAMBLED out of there fast and then out of breath, he sat down in the grass a while and thought of what that sound could be and why hadn't his dog barked? It must be the wind blowing through a tunnel and if that were the case there had to be another way out? So he got up and went back inside the cave entrance, again inching slowly along toward the light. It was shining very dimly up ahead. He heard the moaning sound several times again and again? Then, he and Scrappy came into a much larger opening. There was a small stream of water running along the side of the room-like open space, with a small skylight hole in the top part of the rocks overhead.

"Crazy Crocodiles", he thought. There were also signs of someone having been in here. Glancing all around the open space, he saw a stack of sticks, a pile of blankets, and a place where a small fire had been. Then he saw something and the moaning came again. Over there on the edge of the room something moved. "Something is in here!" He wanted to run out again but he stopped himself because he could see there was a person lying on the blankets. As he caught his breath, his eyes became adjusted even better and he could see it was a man and the guy seemed VERY ill; now he lie very still, maybe he was dying or worse yet already dead… Six feet of earth makes us all equal… It looked like he had been in here a long time. There must be some other people around here? He turned and walked back outside of the cave again, in a bit of shock at what he had found. After looking up and down the area, he saw no sign of anyone else being here? Nagel wasn't sure WHAT to do?

The man must be hiding or maybe he was even a thief and what was wrong with him? Well, he had to be on his way and this was really none of his business.

"I am nobody just one kid out here alone and I need to pack up and get going. Beside what could I DO for that guy? What would Nio do?" he thought to himself. He would have been too smart to go in there in the first… What you do when no one is looking is who you really are…

I could try and see how bad this guy is and ask him if he can get water, before I leave? There is water in the cave but I don't think he can get too it. His thoughts continued. If I do nothing he is as good as DEAD! He checked on Boots, walked around a while and got up his nerve and went back in. He took the water bag with him. The man looked right at him but with unseeing eyes.

Nagel asked him, "Who are you and what are you doing in here?" There was no answer. Nagel's heart was pounding hard but he inched closer, raised the man's head and helped him get a drink, which he swallowed eagerly. Then he saw one of the man's legs was swollen and probably infected with several open sores on it. It was cold in here and a bit of a mess. He could drag over some of that wood to build a fire, clean the room up and leave some of his food behind. That might help this poor guy out a little, he thought. When he came back the man had braced himself up weakly into a half sitting position and he held forth a shaking hand and said,

"Thank you so much for your help! My name is Ethan, I am from Egypt; I am a priest and teacher. Long pause here I- I- have been having a little trouble. Then breathing deeply he added. What is your name and who are you traveling with son?"

"My name is Nagel, I am from Nippur, on my way home, I am by myself with just my dog and a burro, replied Nagel.

Nagel did not get back to Nippur for a loooonngg time. What started out, as a helping hand became a wonderful learning experience for Nagel! Ethan, it was Lord Ethan, he was a man in his early forties he had taught in the Pharaoh's palace in Egypt. He had studied all the known mysteries and mythologies of the gods of Egypt and the Empire of Babylon as well. Having been trained in the entire prodigal, rituals, and ceremonies of the kings, he was a well-educated man. He also knew the stories of Moses and the Children of Israel and what had happened during those years of captivity in Egypt. His changing new philosophies had backfired and now he was a hunted man. In his last skirmish with those opposing him, an arrow had hit his right thigh and he came here to hide out and hopefully to recover from the wound. But his food had run out, and an infection set In the leg and things were getting a little rough. He had a lot of sympathetic friends in the nearby town of Gad but they were hiding undercover also, and didn't even know where he was or if he was still alive.

$$\infty$$

Meanwhile back in Setca, King Lugan was raising horses. Master Armen had brought him even more of them and continued to spend some time with helping to train the younger ones. Sara was becoming an excellent rider. The men found the sunken canoe but no one knew where the two fugitives had gone. Sara never mentioned that she had helped them. But she also didn't know what had happened to them? She often sang the song Nagel had taught her about "Sweet Sara", and continued to think of all the good times that they had together when he was here. She knew she could never forget Nagel! Sometimes she rode by herself to the mountain that they had climbed together.

$$\infty$$

Even though Jarro was blind he soon became in charge of Master Armen's leather shop. He taught the men how to carve, stitch, lace and beautifully decorate the saddles and bridles, but he also continued to make sandals to sell on his own in the street markets of town. Mirna missed Nagel the most. She looked down the palm-treed lane every morning expecting to see him with his dog, on his way home, coming around to greet her at the big kitchen door. But he didn't come.

$$\infty$$

Nagel, Scrappy and Boots went to and from the small nearby town of Gad quite often to buy food and supplies. (He never saw the two rouges again but he kept a wary lookout for them.) No one knew him in Gad and Lord Ethan had enough money to buy everything they needed, and that included learning material for him as well. In fact the cave was becoming overloaded with fire fuel, blankets, clothes and everything they needed and some things they just wanted. He had his own private teacher and what an expert Lord Ethan was on nearly everything.

Nagel worked hard to take good care of Lord Ethan even massaging his leg when it was too painful. They became best of friends with a deep bond of studying together and trying to understand about many of the deeper mysteries of life. *Love is blind but friendship just closes its eyes.*

Lord Ethan said, "God put me in your way Nagel, and having compassion like you did for me, is never out of style.

Lord Ethan noticed the Silver Whistle hanging around Nagel neck and asked about it. When they tested it on several occasions, they decided it was more of a magic feather or lucky rabbit's foot type of thing (the rabbit's foot wasn't very lucky for the rabbit). The next day Nagel threw the Whistle into the nearby creek. Maybe he had outgrown it? Perhaps the old lady's advice, "don't let your past hold you future hostage," had been the most valuable thing she had given him after all.

The wound was healing very slowly and Lord Ethan still could not walk with out help. He dragged himself painfully along using a crutch they had made together. No one had told Nagel when to be home; besides they probably didn't know if he was dead or alive by this time. So do what you have to do, he thought to him self. Lord Ethan needed him desperately right now.

Sometimes they sat in the sun on the grassy hillside and studied together and then just talked. "Nagel there are no shortcuts to maturity." said Lord Ethan

Sometimes they sat inside working by candlelight. NOTE: They had no books, not even papyrus manuscripts; the only method of writing was using symbols (no alphabet was created yet) on a clay tablet. Even these clay tablets needed to be explained to someone who was learning. Most of the communication was word of mouth or passed on stories. Lord Ethan had heard the stories of Abraham, Isaac, Jacob and Joseph and he told and retold them to Nagel. The concept of ONE God was shocking and hard to understand. Nagel had been told of many gods and confusing mystic concepts on how the world came to be. An all-powerful, all knowing, and all present God, sounded too good to be true. If you believed that, you could forget about all the superstitions and curses that often controlled your thinking and actions as well. He was quite fascinated by the Stories of Moses and all the slaves escaping from the Pharaoh (Ramses ll), of Egypt and the many wonders that God had performed. Then the plagues and parting of the Red Sea was mind-boggling.

It didn't happen overnight but Nagel was learning so much and he loved it. He learned of the most fascinating prophecy that was yet to be fulfilled. It was, "that a man greater then all the prophets would come and he would teach about love and kindness and how to live. He would also die for ALL and rise up and be ALIVE again." Nagel longed to still be living when that happened!

One day Nagel asked about the beautiful polished ash wood bow Lord Ethan had placed carefully up on a rock shelf inside their homelike cave. Nagel had never learned how to shoot a bow.

Lord Ethan said, "Come on Nagel, I'll bet we can make an expert archer out of you! That is if you really want to." Oh, he wanted to because it looked like fun but it just wasn't that easy. Nagel was days and days chasing and finding arrows, also making new ones. Several times he gave up and then he wouldn't even try. His arms were too sore. He felt like he just couldn't do it. After all, he wasn't who Sara and many others thought he was (Master Armen's son) he was a Nobody. Why was life so hard? Why did everything you tried to do hurt? He sat down on a rock and just felt sorry for himself. All the mean, unjust things that had ever happened to him in his past swirled around in his mind. Could Sara ever really love him? He sat thinking for a long time. Then Jarro came to mind. Where did Jarro get the courage, and Mirna, her life wasn't easy? He thought of the story of the muskrat the one who tried smarter and made it to shore because he never quit and the old lady who gave him the magic whistle, she died with a smile on her face. If he were just a Nobody he would be the best nobody there ever was. Life was NOT easy, it took courage, and Master Armen was counting on him to keep his promise. He knew Mirna and Jarro really did care about him. He pet and talked to Scrappy for quit a while and then picked up the bow and arrows…

If Sara was ever going to love him he could not be a quitter and he needed to have some manly knowhow!

Lord Ethan was a fabulous shot with the bow and he showed Nagel again how to do it the right way. If you slowly and evenly pull back the bowstring as you bring it into the line of sight, concentrate on where that arrow is to go, by releasing the string slowly with a whisper of a touch you can shoot a bird on the wing. They soon had quail for dinner! After several months of working hard with the bow, Nagel developed bigger and stronger muscles across his chest and down his arms, and he soon became a worthy archery competitor even for Lord Ethan! He also learned to throw an axe and hit a target thirty of forty feet away. He was beginning to feel better about himself but the deep longing to find his roots were still very strong.

One night he confided in Lord Ethan about his lost childhood and the feeling of not being able to express his emotions and NEVER being able to cry. He also told him of the reoccurring dream, the dream with all the white feathers.

"Nagel you need to go and find out what happened that day and find your family if you possible can. Don't let this be a shadow over you," said Lord Ethan. Then he told him about what Jarro had said on that day in Nippur when there was the sudden rainstorm. "The strange woman in the white dress that had been following him, she was most likely from Big Bend."

"You must go and search for her," continued Lord Ethan, "I have some friends in Gad that just might be able to help you."

And so the plan was begun. Nagel had to find the friends of Lord Ethan in Gad first, and inform them of his circumstances. Hopefully, with their help, Lord Ethan could travel to Gad and be cared for while there by his friends and continue to heal. The very first thing Nagel had to do was go to the temple in Gad and find the older priest named Jeddah and quietly, in secret, tell him who sent him. The priest would help him to find the friends. Then later, Lord Ethan would make a detailed map for him of how to get to Big Bend. Nagel would get the supplies for the trip and he, Scrappy, and probably Boots, would GO!

It all worked quite well and Nagel was soon on his way. He had purchased some fine new clothes and had his hair trimmed and he was a strong, tall and very handsome young man by this time. His straight brown hair was shiny and his body was growing enough to match his big feet. This was something he had dreamed of doing so many times. He was a little nervous about it but very excited also! He, Scrappy, and Boots, (who was heavily packed for the trip), left the town of Gad, with a group that would travel with him all the way to the river. From The Tigress River (or a branch of it) he would leave his burro (Boots) at a stable and he and Scrappy would catch a boat going on up stream.

When they finally walked into Big Bend, he already had the feelings of having been there before. The little town sat along the side of a huge curving sandbar on the river, and thus the name Big Bend. It was quite a unique spot and it hadn't changed that much.

Nagel vaguely remembered playing down there, where those white swans were swimming along the beach, with his toy clay boat. His feeling of excitement was building. He RECOGNIZED this place. He knew what to do, at least he thought he did, everyone back in Gad had a different idea of what to do and how to research the story. It had been nearly thirteen years or so as he thought about it. Some of the white swan feathers were drifting in the current of the river.

If he could find someone who had been living here at that time maybe they would remember the incident. Well, after talking for several days to some older folks, things didn't look too promising. Maybe he had come all this way for nothing. But the word was out that a young man in town was searching for his parents. It seemed many people had been living here at that time but each remembered it a bit differently and roving bandits had come to town more then once in the last few years.

Then the next day; "I know who you are and I know who your mother is," replied an older woman.

"Oh what was your name?"

"My name is Nagel." He answered, while staring at her intently.

"Yes that is it, Nagel, you are Nagel! I remember you when you were just a little boy!" She got very excited and began to run up and down and back and forth in her joy of discovery.

"People have been on the lookout for you for years hoping you hadn't died in that terrible massacre that happen about fourteen years ago. It happened right down there, she continued, down by the water and your father was killed right over there," she pointed her finger and waved her hand. Then she glanced up at his face.

"Oh dear me, you didn't KNOW your father was killed that day? I- I- I- wasn't there," she stammered, "I wasn't there when it happened but you wait right here and I'll go and get your mother, Rose."

"No please, lady, just wait!" He stated, and then he found a bench near by and wearily sat down. It was not supposed to happen like this. He had pictured it all sooo differently. But the lady was already gone trotting up the street. Suddenly a wave of fatigue washed over him. Maybe the answers were too much to bear.

The lady came back in about an hour. Nagel was still sitting there on the bench with Scrappy beside him; he looked a bit dazed.

She sat down beside him a while and then said, "Your mother doesn't believe me, or else she is just too shocked. I don't know which it is, but she said for you to come to her house in the morning then she would meet you and talk to you about it. I will be glad to meet you here in the morning and take you up there, if you like?"

"Oh yes, Thank you, I would be pleased if you could do that," he stated. The next morning, Nagel had no idea of what to expect as he and the older lady, walked up the lane. It was an average neighborhood and the house was nice with three rooms and a kitchen on the back, a typical adobe brick.

He looked around trying to remember being here, everything had changed a bit. A small dog and some children's toys were in the front yard. There was a woman and two small children standing in the door watching them approach. She looked kind of like the woman he had seen in the rainstorm that day, or did she? She seemed much shorter, all of a sudden he couldn't seem to remember anything. Maybe he should NOT have come here. Right now, she just stood there, as he stepped up to the doorway, she wouldn't look at him.

Then she said, "Come in" and then she went to the backside of the room and sat down, slowly. He stepped inside and feeling awkward, he just stood there. For several long minutes the room was heavy with silence. All the years of wanting to know and now he felt like his heart was sinking to the floor. The two children sat besides her staring intently at him.

"Nagel, Nagel! Is that really you?" she said in a slow, soft voice shaking with emotion. "Yes MOM it is! I have come back home!" Then they were in each other's arms, hugging, laughing and then crying. CRYING, Nagel was CRYING! The tears just kept rolling down his cheeks and he didn't even TRY to stop them!

He stayed several months with them. He met his stepfather who was a boat builder and worked down near the river. He had a half sister and an even younger half brother. Rose was so amazed at how her little son had grown into such a fine, handsome young man. He was very knowledgeable and capable and even skilled in many things. She told him all the details of what had happened that terrible morning. He was at the waters edge playing with the white swan feathers when it started and how his father had been killed, and he, Nagel had been wounded in the back. He showed her the scar on his back and how he couldn't remember how it got there. Together they went over all his questions about it. Then he told her all about the many special people and adventures that had happened in his life. They talked and talked for days as she recounted the entire happenings in her life also. As you can imagine it went on and on. She also made him several outfits of clothes like his white tunic that he had loved to wear. Who was this tall, handsome stranger, and yet she knew him well, because people are whom they are inside and seldom change… *A rose, is a rose, is a rose!* …She knew his heart and he hers.

They were a happy family but he knew that he and Scrappy, who the children loved to play with, didn't really belong here. He had finally COME HOME and now he must go away again. Maybe he could come back some day but there were a lot of things out there he still had to do. He explained about his promise to Master Armen and his friend whom he had come to love; Lord Ethan in Gad, who was still very sick, and who had taught him so very much. He also told her all about Princess Sara in Setca and how much he wanted to see her again. Later, she showed him his little clay boat and sandals which she had saved all these years. He remembered them and many other things he began to recall as well. Now he understood the dream of the white feathers and many of the missing pieces in his life began to fit together. He was very sad that his father had died but he was finally satisfied with knowing pretty much all of what had happened that terrible morning all those years ago. He didn't feel like a Nobody anymore.

Chapter Fifteen

When he finally returned to Gad he was greeted with horrible news. Lord Ethan had died! They had discovered that a broken piece of the arrow was still in his leg; and when the healer they called, tried to remove it, Lord Ethan had become much worse. There was nothing anybody could do as he gradually weakened and died.

"If only I had been here or maybe if we had not moved him here. Why did I leave him?" It was hard for Nagel not to blame himself for what had happened.

That evening Nagel went out alone to see the grave and then he cried again. This time he stood there in the rain and shook his fists at the sky and sobbed out loud with all the tears of a lifetime running out in a flood. Then the last rays of sunlight broke through the dark clouds and he watched while the glowing lights slowly went down. He remembered more of Lord Ethan's sayings-*Sunset in one place is Sunrise in another*- He had learned real sorrow and how to cry. If we live long enough sorrow comes to ALL of us…*Very heavy slow sad music here…*

Lord Ethan had left several things for him. The beautiful ash wood bow with all the arrows, some of the writings they had made together and money. Also, to his surprise, among the collection of things left for him was the slightly bent Silver Whistle. Someone had found it and saved it for him. It reminded him of Sara so he put it back on.

Lord Ethan

Rose (Mom)

There was also a message: "My dearest Nagel you have been like a shinning light to me, a life-saving friend who stopped to help a man he didn't even know. It has been my joy to train you and teach you many things but the greatest things were already within yourself. You must not hang on to all the wrongs that have followed you in your life. Believe in the honest, caring man you have become in spite of it. Keep my teachings and love in your heart always. May God be with you and richly bless you," signed Lord Ethan. There was more then enough money to see him back to Nippur.

Then Nagel recalled again the words of the older lady that gave him the Magic Whistle... *Don't let your past hold your future hostage...*

Nagel had stopped to get Boots on the return trip from Big Bend but she was in foal and ready to deliver and so he left her as payment for her board.

He knew he was an older, wiser person as he returned to Nippur. He and Scrappy went first of all to see Jarro. Most of the people he had known while living on the streets had moved on somewhere else and of those still there some didn't even remember him.

They told him about Maromset falling in love with a rabbit in a cage and leaving town with the animal trainer. That was not much of a surprise, but the real surprise came, when he heard that Jarro at least part time, now lived and worked at Master Armen's place.

Would he be a HERO or a VILLIAN when he walked down that familiar palm-treed lane to Master Armen's place? He thought to himself, trials could be God's way to triumpth. No matter, he did what he felt he had to do and now he would keep his PROMISE and return even if he became a slave again forever. There was a sales merchant's wagon making a delivery. Erron, the yard keeper had the big wooden gates open. Nagel burst through unannounced and slipped in through the open gates. Erron looked surprised but just let him pass through. The dogs began barking at him, just as they usually did. He walked down the stone path with the beautiful blue tile and through the flower garden and around to the back and into Mirna's kitchen. She calmly looked up at him with a big smile and gave him the biggest hug with a kiss.

"Where have you been? You are late! I KNEW you would come back!" Then she dried her tears of joy. Jarro was equally overjoyed to see him and to know he had safely returned.

When all of the excitement of his return had calmed down a little bit and the many stories were told and retold, he told Master Armen how much Nio had helped him while at Setca and when and how they escaped, and that he (Nio) had just left, later, while on the trip home. But he didn't tell just when and where this happened, so as not to cause any trouble for Nio. He learned that Master Armen and all the men HAD returned on TIME to free him and Nio. Master Armen had kept his PROMISE!

Then Master Armen planned a big celebration in Nagel's honor. It was truly a grand affair with nearly everyone Nagel knew, even some of the street people, plus much nobility were present; even the King of Nippur (Tukulti-ninurta) was invited. The king himself wanted to hear all the stories first hand from the beginning of the Lion Hunt to the adventures at the Setca oasis and so forth. Nagel was seated in a place of honor beside Master Armen at the big table. After the wonderful banquet dinner, entertainment, and even more story telling, Nagel was asked to step up to the Royal platform beside Master Armen.

"Nagel", Master Armen began speaking loudly so all could hear, "what you have done by staying behind in Setca and allowing the rest of us to go home may have saved all our lives that day and I wish to honor you for doing so. Not only that, you kept your PROMISE to never run away again and you came back on your own. Stand up here beside me son, for you truly are a son to me and never again will you be a street boy or slave! You will, as my adopted son, be free to come and go as you please and share in all my wealth. As a special present to honor you, I am giving you this gold ring with the Armen symbol on it, plus my favorite Black stallion!" He grabbed Nagel by the hand and gave it a big shake. "You can have the little brown mare also if you like." Then the "Welcome Home" ceremony ended with a big tearful hug from Master Armen.

Later that evening, Nagel was presented with a saddle blanket designed with the Armen symbol on it, as well as a beautiful new saddle and bridle made by Jarro who was also at the banquet. There were many hugs and kisses and Nagel was smiling a lot!

"I want to present you to the King of Nippur in the land of Babylonia and all our guests here tonight as, Nagel of the Armen Estate, my newly adopted so!"

"Thank you very much Master Armen, I am truly honored," Nagel stated. He stood there looking around at the many people he knew and loved in the room, (he was taller then Master Armen now) but inside he thought, "I really DID keep my promise didn't I? This was a bit too much; he knew how close he had come to messing things up on so many occasions. I could never have stayed in Setca as a hostage without the help of my friend Nio, and we could never have escaped with out the help of Sara." So many people had helped to shape his life. Without Lord Ethan he could not have found his mother, Rose, and gotten back home to Nippur. It had been a long road he traveled and he would never forget what he had learned and the many people he had met along the way. He could not cry "poor me" anymore. It was time to grow up! Nagel was not just a Nobody! He had learned to laugh and he had learned to cry, and now he even had a place to belong. But he had not acquired a gift of gab and he didn't know what more to say! Out came a soft but sincere.

"Thank you, thank you ALL very much!"

Ahan, Master's son, was a bit jealous but he felt even more of a feeling of awe and admiration of how much Nagel had changed and the adventures he had experienced. Plus the skills he had acquired. Ahan was surprised when Nagel graciously offered to spend some time out hunting with him. He never again challenged him to an archery contest, when he saw what an excellent, skilled archer Nagel had become. Wow, even his new step-brother was starting to like him. It must be time to leave already.

Then one morning Master Gates met him on the back porch and said, "Nagel, I need to talk to you. I never thought you would make it back or keep your promise the way you did, but I am happy that you did. He continued speaking very softly.

"You see I have a son of my own."

"Yes I know, said Nagel." Gates jerked his head around in surprise.

"Oh, it was you that followed me that night, that night I took the little white cat"

"Yes it was me and I saw your son and I would like to meet him, stated Nagel."

"Then you shall," said Master Gates, with a slow smile coming onto his long thin face. The young bed-ridden man's name was Samuel and the two quickly became good friends. Nagel went to see him often. *I felt sorry for myself because I had no shoes until I met a man who had no feet…*

Samuel was quite taken with the Magic Whistle and learned to blow it very well with Nagel's help. Nagel gave it to him as a present the day before he left Master Armen's Estate.

Several months had passed and Nagel told everyone goodbye. Then he loaded up the black stallion (with the pretty Armen banner blankets and the new saddle made by Jarro) and packed up the little brown mare and carefully tied on the now very special Lion skin. With Scrappy trotting along side, Nagel again rode out through the big wooden gates and on through the streets of Nippur. He traveled along the same trail they started on the morning of the Lion Hunt. He was dressed in one of his favorite white tunics (made by his mother, Rose) and he carried a quiver full of arrows and the ash wood bow strung across his broad shoulders. There was a shining gold ring on his finger. Nagel had kept his PROMISE and then some. It was more then just the satisfaction of finding his home and having all the friends and admiration. He realized he did not feel angry and alone anymore. He had discovered a higher power God loved him and would direct him in his life. If he would just listen to the still small voice inside his heart, he could know right from wrong and he would never really be ALONE!

He was thinking, "You CAN change your destiny!" He had unfinished business and "Crazy Crocodiles!" He knew WHO he was and WHERE he was from and WHERE he was going! He was NAGEL, the seeker, from ancient Babylonia. Arriving at one goal is the starting point of another…*This one thing I do, forgetting those things that are behind and reaching forth to those things that are before, I press toward the mark… Philippians 3:13&14*

. His white LION BOY boots had worn out long ago but he knew where to get a new pair! He also wanted to return that last gold coin that Sara had put in the little leather pouch. It was carefully wrapped and tucked deeply in his pocket. Mirna had always told him. *It is in loving, not in being loved, that the heart is blessed; it is in giving, not in receiving, that we find our quest.* King Lugan would need to know the truth about who he really was. He pictured himself standing tall and looking down at the short but fearsome King. Could he tell all of them who he really was and what had happened and why he had returned? YES, if he could just FIND the place, he knew he COULD and would!

As he rode along, he remembered the bent Silver Whistle and smiled at the thought of when beautiful sweet Sara had put the cork in the bottom and played a tune on it. Was she still there in beautiful Setca? Would she remember him? This would be a whole new chapter in his life, but he really didn't need any more Magic Whistles, besides, he knew how to make a beautiful flute out of bamboo. Jarro had taught him so many things.

He urged the black stallion into a fast swinging walk with the little brown mare following behind and Scrappy in the lead. It was spring and what a BEAUTIFUL morning it was! As he crossed that same small wooden bridge the hoof sounds again echoed out across the water just as they had years before on that fateful morning of the Lion Hunt. As Nagel looked out across the wide, shining river, he wondered what this venture might lead him too. What ever happened, right now he felt light hearted with an inner surge of confidence. He begins to sing out in a deep mellow voice, along with the swinging rhythm of the horse's hoof beats. *"Down in some green valley in a lonesome place where the wild birds do whistle and their notes do increase. Farwell pretty Sara I bid you adieu but I'll dream of pretty Sara wherever I go."*

Beautiful, grand flowing adventure
type music played right along with him!

The End

In loving memory of my son
James Steven Rolls
June 22, 1952—September 3, 1961

To you, O Lord, I lift up my soul:
in you I trust, O my God.

Psalm 25:1-2